# SAINT PIUS X
## THE FARM BOY WHO BECAME POPE

# SAINT PIUS X
## THE FARM BOY
## WHO BECAME POPE

*Written by Walter Diethelm, O.S.B.*

Illustrated by G. W. Thompson

IGNATIUS PRESS    SAN FRANCISCO

Cover design by Riz Boncan Marsella
Cover illustration by Christopher J. Pelicano

Published by Ignatius Press, San Francisco, 1994
All rights reserved
ISBN 978-0-89870-469-3
Library of Congress catalogue number 93-78530
Printed in the United States of America

# CONTENTS

# I

# THE YOUNG STUDENT

G IOVANNI SARTO made his rounds through the narrow streets of the farm village of Riese. He noticed neither the burning sun nor the weight of the mail bag on his shoulder. All he could think of was the talk he had had with his son the night before. "I would like to become a priest", young

7

Giuseppe—whom they all called Bepi—had confided.

A priest! How Giovanni thrilled at the thought of giving a son to God! But eleven-year-old Bepi was the eldest son, and Giovanni had been looking forward to the day when he would finish school and would be able to help out at home. Even with his work as janitor and messenger, Papa Sarto made only fifty cents a day. It wasn't easy to support a family of eight children on such a salary, even though food was not as expensive in Italy in 1846 as it is now. But soon, he had thought, Bepi would help.

"Hi, Gian!" Sarto almost jumped as he heard his nickname called out. "Any mail for us?"

"Nothing today, Antonio."

"I was just saying to my wife, Gian, that your Bepi is a boy to be proud of. It isn't very often that practically all the school prizes are won by a single boy. It's too bad he can't continue in school for a few more years. He's a bright one!"

And Giovanni Sarto's problem became even more unbearable as he replied. "I know, Antonio. If only our village school could give more than two years of learning, perhaps I could afford to keep him in school. But Castelfranco is the nearest town with a senior elementary school, and that is four miles away—a long distance for a boy to walk each day."

Bepi's father was thinking, too, of the learning a priest must have—learning that one could not begin to get at the village school of Riese. And then he thought again of his own advancing age, of the family at home, and of how much he needed the help Bepi could give.

With a wave and a sympathetic "We all have our problems, Gian", Antonio was off. Giovanni Sarto shifted his mail bag and walked on.

Yes, indeed, thought Sarto, his Bepi *was* a son to be proud of—tall, straight, and strong, with steady blue eyes like his mother's. Bright and friendly he was, and happy—but he could use his fists, too, and Papa chuckled as he thought of the problems Bepi had settled that way.

Giovanni, now at the end of his route, tipped his cap and whispered a prayer as he passed the church. This was a lesson he had early taught his children; and they had learned it well. Bepi, after playing an exciting game of ball, never failed to dash into church before going home, kneel before the Blessed Sacrament, and pray as fervently as he had been playing ball.

As he passed the rectory, Giovanni Sarto suddenly knew the very one to give him good advice about Bepi—the pastor, Don Tito. After all, when it's a question of becoming a priest, he decided, not only God—but God's servant, too—should have a say in the matter.

The first thing Don Tito said to Sarto in the rectory was a joy for the father to hear.

"Bepi is the brightest boy in the parish. His catechism marks have always been the highest in his class. Why, just the other day, in class, he amazed me with a really brilliant comment. I had said, 'I will give an apple to anyone who can tell me where God is.' And your Bepi replied, 'I will give two apples to anyone who can tell me where God isn't.' A remarkably intelligent boy!

"Yes," the priest went on, "if God has chosen one child out of the lot to be a priest, then Bepi is certainly the one. His love of God is strong, and he is never happier than when he is serving Mass. You know yourself how overjoyed he was a few months ago when he received his First Holy Communion."

Giovanni Sarto nodded and pondered, never dreaming that his Bepi would someday sit in the Chair of Peter as the humble and beloved Pope Pius X. As "the Pope of little children", he would see to it that never again would children be made to wait, as he had, until the age of eleven to receive our Lord in the Holy Eucharist. First Holy Communion, he would rule, was to take place as soon as the child was old enough to understand what was meant by the solemn occasion.

But Giovanni Sarto, as he rose from the creaking chair, never dreamed of such a life for his son. He grasped the pastor's hand and made his decision. "I need Bepi. But if God wants him, God shall have him."

For the next four years, Bepi attended school in Castelfranco. Through wind and rain, through snowstorms and heat, he made the journey. And he never complained; he was happy to be able to go to school awhile longer in preparation for his high calling.

Sarto the student attracted attention both in the town of Castelfranco and at school. He was a cheerful, friendly boy, well-liked by everyone. Each morning after Mass he would trudge along the dusty road to Castelfranco, his books over his shoulder, calling a greeting to everyone he met.

Usually there was something else slung over Bepi's shoulder too—his pair of shoes. He had once heard his mother sigh, "Shoes cost so much." And Bepi had understood at once. He knew that when there are so many children in a family, it costs a lot to make sure that each one has a pair of shoes to wear, at least on Sundays. So Bepi saved his shoes by walking barefoot on the road between his home town and Castelfranco. When he reached the gates of the town, he would put on his shoes.

At school, Bepi was not like the other boys, most of whom came from the town. Next to him sat boys from well-to-do families. Some of the students were even the sons of noblemen, and these boys were already leading a gentleman's life. One of them tells of the impression that the poor country boy from Riese made on him: "He was very poorly dressed, and sometimes you could see the piece of bread that he had brought for his lunch, peeking out of his pocket. But he was so good! Everybody loved him. He was so happy and he worked very hard. At school he was always first in his class. Every month the school arranged the names of the pupils in the order of their scholastic standing. The record was framed and posted for all to see. At the end of the year we would all go to the nearby town of Treviso to take our examination. Bepi always came out first!"

The tax collector of Castelfranco was a friend of Papa Sarto, and each day at noon Bepi would go to the home of this good man and his wife. There he would eat the lunch he had brought with him from Riese. And we can well imagine that many a time the tax collector's wife, her heart aching at the thought of Bepi's meager lunch, made sure that her cookie jar was extra full.

During vacations, Bepi would serve Mass in the morning, and then he would often lead a group of neighborhood children to an outdoor shrine of our Lady. There they would recite her litany and sing hymns.

When Bepi was in his fourth and last year at Castelfranco, he was joined by his brother Angelo. Bepi had been earning money by tutoring other pupils, and the family by this time could afford to send Angelo to Castelfranco to go to school with Bepi.

Every day the two boys had to walk for an hour and a half to get to school. After a while, their father bought them a little wagon and a donkey to pull it. Of course, the wagon wasn't new and the donkey wasn't young, but the boys didn't mind when the old cart rattled along, creaking and groaning in every joint. The main thing was that they no longer had to go by foot!

A man from Riese, who often met them on the way, has given us a vivid picture of them: "It was a pleasure to see them drive by. Every now and then there would be a little argument because both of them wanted to play at being coachman. But Bepi always won. He would stand up straight in the cart like a Roman charioteer, lift his stick in a threatening way, pull the reins tight, shout at the top of his voice, and drive the little donkey ahead so as to be sure of getting to school on time."

It is easy to picture this little country boy from Riese who knows how to keep a firm hand on the reins when there is something to steer or to lead. He is no clumsy fellow with whom you can do as you like. Later on, too, he will know how to take matters firmly in hand, and then he will have more important things to direct than an old, rattling cart drawn by a donkey.

Now and then donkeys have a way of being stubborn. More than once on the drive to school, the Sarto donkey would go on strike and refuse to move. At these times, the patience of the two Sarto boys wore thin, for neither of them wanted to miss a minute of school. Their fellow students tell us that every now and then the two Sarto brothers would arrive late, in spite of their efforts to hurry their donkey.

Bepi had his childish faults. It is said that he had quite a temper. Luckily, he had a wonderful mother who knew very well how to help her Bepi chase away his temper-devil. She had one cure that never failed to work. When her son began to boil with rage, she needed only to look at him with her warm, kind eyes, and his anger always cooled down quickly.

When Bepi Sarto was fifteen, he had successfully completed the four classes of school at Castelfranco. At the end of the last year, there was a big final examination in which forty-three students took part. But it was not the city boys who won the prizes, and it wasn't the sons of the nobility. At the head of the list was a country boy from Riese, Bepi Sarto. He was the only one to get the highest grade in every single subject. And yet he was the one who had the least time to study. For when he got home every day from his long trip to school, he had to pitch in and help with the chores. He had to take care of the stable, carry mail for his father, herd the cattle if he had a free afternoon, and attend to a thousand other things that would help lift the burden of work from the shoulders of his mother and father.

## II

## THE SEMINARIAN

THAT EVENING, Bepi the prize-winner, who should have been able to rush home full of joy to announce his great success to his parents, trudged back slowly, weighed down by worry. How can I go on studying? he kept asking himself anxiously. He had finished the course in Castelfranco.

"I must go on and study more", he thought. "I must go to the seminary at Padua. But who will pay for that? Certainly not Father. He has enough to worry about just seeing to it that everybody at home has enough to eat."

In his confusion and discouragement, Bepi did exactly what his father had done four years earlier. He went to see the pastor and told him his troubles.

"Show me your marks", the priest said.

Bepi gave him his report card, and Don Tito read it through, slowly and thoughtfully.

"That's a good report," he comforted the boy, "a very good report! See . . . God has helped you until now. He will continue to help you. And I will see what I can do for you myself. But you must do something too. In the days to come, you must get down on your knees, Bepi! You and your family must pray and have faith. Surely God has some plan in mind for you."

During the days that followed, Bepi prayed as he had never prayed before in all his life. For he knew very well that his whole future, his vocation for the priesthood, depended on his prayers. Every day he made a visit to the nearby shrine of the Mother of God, where he implored the Queen of Heaven to give him her motherly help.

During these same days, Don Tito wrote a letter. He knew that it was the privilege of the cardinal archbishop of Venice to dispose of several scholarships for free schooling and board at the seminary of Padua. These scholarships were awarded to deserving boys whose parents could not afford to pay their expenses. It happened that the cardinal was himself a native of Riese. If he wrote to the cardinal, thought Don Tito, and explained Bepi's problem, one of the scholarships might be awarded to young Sarto. Surely the cardinal would recall his own childhood in Riese when, as Jacopo Monico—son of the blacksmith—he had so longed to be a priest. In his home, too, the necessary money had been lacking. How overjoyed he had been when he had received a scholarship to study at the seminary!

When Don Tito had sent off his letter, Bepi's family prayed even harder than before. The mother prayed, for every good mother longs to have her son become a priest. The father prayed; whenever he passed a wayside crucifix on his mail carrier's route, he would stand still, fold his hands, and pray "Lord, may everything turn out for the best."

But Bepi prayed more than anyone. He made one novena after another, and it seemed to him that the cardinal's reply would never come. Men in high positions get a great many letters and do not have time to answer all their mail right away. And so the letter from Riese lay waiting in Venice for four weeks before the cardinal wrote.

Every morning after he had served Mass, Bepi waited for Don Tito to ask him to come to the rectory. But, again and again, the good priest only shook his head. That meant that His Eminence, the cardinal, had not yet written! One day, however, the priest showed Bepi the long-awaited letter.

"Come and see me in the rectory, Bepi, and I will read you what His Eminence, the cardinal, has written us."

The letter from Venice contained such good news that Bepi turned a handspring right in the rectory living room. Then he hurried home to give the good news to his family.

"Papa! Mama! I've been given a scholarship to study at the School of Divinity at Padua. And I must be there by the thirteenth of November!"

Padua! Every Italian child thrills at that name. Saint Anthony, the famous worker of miracles, the universal helper, once lived in that city. There he died and there—in one of the most splendid churches—he lies buried. And Bepi was to go to Padua to enter the seminary. At first he would attend the preparatory school but, after a while, he would graduate into the School of Divinity itself. He was very happy.

In those days, boys did not wait until they entered the seminary to wear the black cassock. This cassock—an outward mark of the priesthood—was received by the boy from the hands of his own pastor in his home parish before he left for the seminary. And so, a month after the good news had come from the cardinal, the villagers of Riese gathered in the church to watch Don Tito clothe their Bepi in the priestly cassock. His mother wept for joy and insisted that her children treat their brother with all possible respect.

The villagers were proud of their neighbor and anxious to have a share in helping him to become a priest of God. So they quickly contributed a sum of money to help the Sarto family pay Bepi's minor expenses.

In November of 1850, fifteen-year-old Bepi Sarto took one long, fond look around his simple room in the home where he had been born. Then he quickly hugged his mother and climbed into the stagecoach that was to take him to Padua and the first step of his long and saintly life as a priest.

Giuseppe immediately felt at home in the atmosphere of the seminary at Padua. The strict discipline and the hours devoted to prayer and meditation made him feel even closer to God. As a student, he delighted in the difficult work of learning languages, sciences, history, and the classics. He spent hours in the library surrounded by his beloved books. The other seminarians used to say jokingly, "Behind that mountain of books sits Bepi Sarto building a mountain of notes." His friendly, cheerful manner brought him many friends, just as at Castelfranco. He was first in the class of fifty-six students, and at the end of the year, he received this report: "He is second to none when it comes to observing the rules. He is endowed with outstanding intellectual gifts and with an acute mind. We feel justified in expecting great things of him."

In August, Bepi returned home to Riese for vacation. He was welcomed with joy by his family, friends, and the parish priests, Don Tito and Don Pietro. He taught Christian doctrine to the children and attended all devotions in the church. With his family, he spent hours telling of his life in the seminary and listening to all the little bits of news children store up to tell their favorite big brother.

Bepi returned to Padua in the fall to continue the brilliant work he had begun the year before. But his second school year was to bring him a great sorrow.

One night in the spring, young Giuseppe awakened with the strange and terrifying feeling that he was needed at home. He dressed and went to the rector's room.

"Please, Father, I must go home at once. My father is very ill."

"Your father?" the superior asked in astonishment. "Has a messenger been here with bad news from your home?"

"There has been no messenger, Father, but I know it is true. Please, may I go?"

Had it been any other pupil, the rector might have shaken his head and thought: Either this boy wants to escape some classes or he's homesick. He's made up this story to get a few extra holidays. But no one could think such a thing of Giuseppe Sarto. So he was given permission to visit his home for a few days. Bepi got there just in time. He found his father in bed, very ill. In spite of devoted care, he died only a few days later.

After his father had been buried, Bepi was faced with a difficult decision. Should he go on studying? On the very day of his father's death, a new baby sister—the tenth child—had arrived in the world. No . . . really there was too much work for his mother to do.

"Mama, I will gladly stay home now and help you", Bepi offered.

But his mother would not accept the sacrifice. "Bepi," she said, "you must never take off your black cassock. You must become a priest if God desires it. We will get along here without you. Angelo is almost seventeen years old now. He can take over the letter-carrying. He's old enough for that. All you have to do is pray. That is the work you can do for us." And Mama Sarto, with the help of her daughters, set about establishing a dressmaking business.

The second summer's vacation was a sad one for Bepi and his family; Papa Sarto was badly missed. In the fall, the young seminarian again looked forward to the prayer and study of his life at Padua. About that time, he wrote to Don Pietro, who had been transferred to another parish: "Though I feel sorry to

see the autumn days pass away, it is my greatest consolation to know that soon I shall be going back to
the seminary where once again I shall find peace and
happiness."

But before young Sarto could begin his third year
in the seminary, he had to obtain money to pay for
his books and incidental expenses. And so he was
forced to beg at the homes of his neighbors in order
to get enough money to return to Padua. But his
natural hesitancy and embarrassment were completely overshadowed by his strong belief that he
*must* become a priest. And the good citizens of
Riese gladly gave what they could to Postman
Sarto's boy.

In 1858, after eight years at Padua, Bepi was close
to his goal. As he finished his course, the rector at
the seminary said of him: "Sarto, in all the eight
years that he has passed in this seminary, has shown
only desirable qualities. He was a constant example
of sincerity, piety, and conduct. I often pray that
God will multiply young men of this type in our
seminaries."

It is a rule of the Church that a young man must
be at least twenty-three years old to be ordained. But
Bepi Sarto finished his course at the seminary eight
months before he was twenty-three. So his superiors
wrote to Rome to obtain special permission for his
ordination. This is called a dispensation. The permission was granted, and on the eighteenth of Septem-

ber, 1858, at Castelfranco, Giuseppe Sarto was ordained a priest.

What a feast there was in little Riese when the young priest came home on the following day to celebrate his first Mass! For everyone knew young Sarto and liked him. All the people had taken pleasure in seeing him when he came home for holidays, each time a little more grown-up and—so it seemed to them—always more lovable and more pious.

Everybody knew his family and especially respected his mother, who for some years now had supported her children without a husband's help. Indeed, many of these people had given their own savings to make sure that this happy day would come.

On that day, Bepi's mother must have been the happiest of all. Her son was now a priest of God. Her prayers and sacrifices had received a rich reward. The good woman must have thought that, for the rest of her life, no day would come for her that could be more beautiful.

# III

# ASSISTANT AT TOMBOLO

ONE EVENING in late autumn, Bepi—who was now called *Don* (or Father) Sarto—sat with his mother in their tiny living room in Riese. But even as she was resting, Mama's needle flew through the bright cotton material she was sewing. She had long before learned never to be idle.

The mother and son, in silence, sat enjoying this moment of being together. Bepi was the first to speak.

"I wanted to wait until the children were in bed, Mama, to tell you this. Today I received my appointment from the bishop. I am to leave for Tombolo to be assistant to Don Antonio in the parish of Saint Andrew."

Mama's eyes, just for a second, showed her sorrow at losing this strong, loving son once more. For, in the weeks since his ordination, his presence had been more of a comfort and joy to his mother than anyone could imagine. But now she rejoiced with Bepi, knowing how anxious he was to begin his work for God and knowing too that this work would be the culmination of all that she and her family had dreamed of for him.

And so Don Giuseppe set out for Tombolo, a small farming village of about 1,200 people. The pastor, Don Antonio, had been ill and unable to do all the work of the parish. He saw at once that the bishop had sent him a true man of the people—a farm boy raised in poverty who would understand his parishioners and draw them to him. One needed only to look at him in his worn coat and wooden-soled shoes, with his sympathetic eyes and strong, gentle hands, to know that here was a priest with a true feeling for his people.

Each morning, Don Sarto rose very early, meditated and prayed before the Blessed Sacrament, and then devoutly celebrated Mass. It is said that some of his parishioners remarked that they felt as if they were seeing Christ himself at the altar, so evident was the sanctity of their priest.

His day was completely devoted to his people. He joked with them, joined in their village games, understood their problems, and consoled and strengthened them. He visited the sick, taught catechism, trained the villagers to sing the Mass, and then returned to his room at night to study and meditate. He was soon able to get along with only four hours of sleep a night.

Don Giuseppe was especially concerned about the young men of his parish. They liked to gamble on street corners. When he happened to come their way, he would sit down and play with them. Sometimes he won a good sum of money; other times he lost. But when he won, he always returned the money to the boys. "The important point for me", he used to say, "is to keep the boys away from bad company while they are playing."

One day he surprised a group of small boys who were playing for money too, like their older brothers. Of course, he sat down and played with them. But after a while the young priest had beaten the children so badly that they had lost all their pennies to him. So he put the pennies in his pocket and started down the street.

"Well, good-bye, boys", he called over his shoulder. "I'll have to get back to the rectory now."

"Wait, Father", they called, as they ran down the

street after him, thinking of their pennies he had in his pocket. Surely he wouldn't keep them. He must have forgotten to give them back.

Don Sarto turned to look at the boys who were following him.

"Yes, what is it, boys?"

"Father, it's about my pennies", one tow-headed, six-year-old finally wailed. "I really need them. I'm supposed to go to the store."

"But you gambled and lost, Pietro. They belong to me now."

The little one looked crushed. And it was then that Don Sarto decided that the children had learned their lesson.

"Very well," he said, "here is your money. But don't let me catch you gambling again. Your parents have worked hard for this money; it is not yours to waste. When you are older and have your own money, you may decide for yourselves whether it is right or wrong for you to use it in this way."

And Don Sarto smiled to himself as the children trooped off to the store, their lesson learned.

Don Sarto spent a great deal of time preparing his sermons. He knew that he must find just the right words to appeal to the farmers and cattle-raisers who were so much like his own neighbors in Riese.

Don Giuseppe, it seems, had a gift for preaching. In fact, when he stood in the pulpit and preached for the first time, all the ladies in the congregation were moved to tears. But Don Antonio was not quite satisfied.

"You did very well," he told his young assistant after the first sermon, "but you can still improve in some ways."

And Don Giuseppe, the man who had always received the best marks in school, nodded his head humbly. He agreed that he should practice his next sermon with the pastor alone in the empty church. But his teacher still found plenty to criticize.

Finally, one Sunday evening, Don Antonio was able to say to his young assistant, "Today, I was entirely satisfied with the way you preached." Then, smiling, he shook a finger at the younger man. "But it's not fitting", he teased, "for the curate to preach better than the pastor."

Don Sarto was troubled because there was so much swearing among the people of Tombolo. Once, when a boy swore in his presence, Don Sarto slapped him on the cheek. Years later, this same boy, when he was told that Don Sarto had been made a bishop, remembered that blow. "I'm not surprised to hear it. When he was still a curate in Tombolo, he 'confirmed' me."

But finally the clever young priest managed to cure the young men completely from swearing. He made a bargain with them. One day a group of young people came to him and said that they wished they could learn to read and write.

"I'll tell you what", Don Giuseppe told them. "We'll start a night school. In the evening when you've finished work, come to the rectory and I'll teach you."

"That's a wonderful idea", one boy exclaimed. "But the trouble is that some of us already know something about reading and writing. How can we all learn in the same class?"

"Don't worry", Don Giuseppe replied. "We'll do it this way: those of you who can already read and write, we'll send to the schoolmaster. The others I'll take on myself."

"How much will we have to pay for our lessons?" asked another young man who was a little more thoughtful than the rest.

"I don't want you to give me any money. But you'll have to give me something else, something that's much more important to me. Stop profaning the name of God with your swearing, and I will feel that I have been well paid."

So the bargain was made. Those big boys whom the curate had taken under his wing and who were still struggling to learn their ABCs shook hands with him and accepted his offer. And they faithfully kept their promise.

Don Giuseppe could well have used some extra money. Neighboring curates, it is said, used to joke about his ragged coat and say the Don Giuseppe must have just come from the war. But he refused to spend money on himself and gave everything he could find to the poor.

One day his sister asked him to buy some sheets for which she had been saving a long time. He took the money but soon returned without the package. He had met some poor children on the way and had given them all the money.

Don Sarto's salary consisted mostly of contributions of corn and wheat from his parishioners. He went from door to door and gratefully accepted whatever the good people gave him. Usually, however, it was not on his own account that he went begging; he went for those who were still poorer than himself.

The pay he had collected never stayed very long with Don Giuseppe. His heart was much too good.

One day a poor man came to his door and asked for money.

"I haven't any money myself", replied the curate.

"Then may I have some corn?" asked the beggar.

The kind-hearted curate unlocked the room where he kept his corn and showed the beggar his whole supply. "We'll divide the corn into equal parts: one part for you, the other for me."

The beggar saw at a glance that he had been given more than he expected. Ashamed of himself, he stammered out his thanks and then quickly picked up his share. And Don Giuseppe was perfectly satisfied with what was left.

Don Sarto's fame as a preacher began to spread

throughout the neighboring towns, and he was often asked to preach in other parishes. But the money he received from this work was soon spent in doing good for the poor.

Once, when Bepi returned from a nearby village after having given a sermon, Don Antonio found that his assistant had not even been able to keep the money until he got home. He had met a poor man on the road and had given it to him.

It happened once that, on their great feast day, the people of the neighboring village of Galliera were very much troubled. The priest who had agreed to give the sermon could not come, and there was no one in the whole neighborhood who felt able to preach the sermon without any preparation.

"Leave the matter to me", the curate, Don Carlo, comforted his pastor. "Don Giuseppe of Tombolo is a good friend of mine. I'm sure he'll help us out."

He jumped into a carriage and arrived just as Don Giuseppe was going into the church to teach catechism.

"Stop! Stop!" Don Carlo called out. "You've got to come to Galliera. The preacher we were expecting can't come."

"What are you thinking of?" Don Giuseppe answered. "Do you think I can just pull a sermon out of thin air?"

"You've simply got to come. Your own pastor orders you to. We haven't a minute to lose!"

As he spoke, the friend from Galliera grabbed the curate by the arm and pulled him into the carriage.

When they arrived at Galliera, Don Carlo took his prisoner into an empty room, gave him paper and pencil, and said to him: "Now I'm going to leave you alone. You have a whole hour. In that time I'm sure you'll be able to put together a fine sermon."

Don Carlo came back in an hour and led Don Giuseppe to the pulpit. The sermon that day was so beautiful that everybody praised the substitute preacher. No one suspected that he had been invited at the last minute. The pastor himself confessed, "In his place, I would not have trusted myself to mount that pulpit. Although I've been a priest for thirty years, I'm sure my sermon would not have turned out so well."

So Bepi's years at Tombolo passed, and it became obvious that Don Antonio had been right. For he had written to a friend long before: "They have sent me as assistant a young priest to direct in the duties of a parish priest; I assure you that the contrary will happen. He is so zealous, so full of good sense and of other precious endowments, that I can learn much from him."

IV

# A FAVOR FOR SALZANO

DON ANTONIO lit his pipe and settled back in front of the fireplace in the rectory at Tombolo. Next to him sat Don Carlo, the neighboring curate, who had stopped for a visit. Don Sarto had just been called out to visit a sick person.

"It's been eight years since Don Giuseppe first came to me", the pastor began. "Those years, like all pleasant ones, have slipped by quickly. He has become as dear to me as a son, and I couldn't wish for a better assistant."

33

"The people love him too", Don Carlo replied. "I have heard them speak of him as their saint. Sometimes they even change the *r* in his name to call him Don *Santo*. It is their way of showing how fond they are of him."

"But, you know, Don Carlo, I worry sometimes about our Bepi. It isn't right that we should keep him all to ourselves here in Tombolo. He is so capable that he could easily manage a big parish. The only thing that surprises me is that he hasn't been promoted long ago. Can the bishop have forgotten about him?"

Don Carlo drew on his pipe contentedly. "I don't think the bishop has forgotten about him. It wasn't very long ago that Don Giuseppe was invited by the bishop to take a teaching position in the seminary. Do you remember what he said when he refused? 'I am a simple country priest. This is where I belong, here among my own kind of people.' I knew he would feel that way about it. But I'm sure the bishop will make Bepi a pastor someday soon."

A few weeks after the two priests had had their talk, a monsignor came from Treviso to visit Saint Andrew's in Tombolo. Treviso was the cathedral city of the diocese. The bishop had his residence in Treviso, and all the business of the diocese was conducted there. The monsignor who visited Tombolo was a canon—that is, he was assigned to the cathedral in order that he might assist the bishop.

Don Antonio saw his opportunity to send back to the bishop news of Bepi's good work. And so the pastor told of his assistant's zeal and sanctity, of his intelligence and humility.

The monsignor rubbed his hands together and thought for a minute.

"There is one very good way of bringing your Don Giuseppe to the bishop's attention. As you know, a famous preacher always delivers the sermon in the cathedral on Saint Anthony's feast day. The bishop is sure to notice this priest, and if your curate is as good as you say, he should be able to deliver that sermon. Do you think he could do it without my feeling ashamed of him?"

"I'm sure of it", the pastor of Tombolo answered.

And so it was that on Saint Anthony's day a tall, thin, haggard-looking figure in a black cassock ascended the great pulpit of the cathedral. The congregation stared up at him in amazement. They had expected to see a bishop or monsignor in purple robes—a preacher well-known for his eloquence.

"Who is that?" they asked one another. No one knew. Finally someone said, "It's the curate from Tombolo."

"Oh, heavens", moaned one woman with disappointment. "Only a simple country priest. Then we're in for a boring talk."

But, after a few moments, everyone in the cathedral was listening intently to this young priest who preached God's word with such warmth and sincerity. They were sorry when his sermon ended more than an hour later.

The bishop, too, was listening and thinking, "Anyone who preaches like that—with such simplicity and charity—would certainly make a good pastor. I must try to find this country curate a position that will give his talents a better chance to develop."

Only a few weeks later, Don Giuseppe Sarto was appointed to be pastor of the town of Salzano. The young priest was overwhelmed, and he threw himself before the altar, praying *Domine non sum dignus*— Lord, I am not worthy. But his first duty was obedience, so Don Giuseppe sorrowfully packed his few possessions and said good-bye to his dear people of Tombolo. They all grieved to see him go, but Don Antonio was particularly downcast. "What have I started?" he wailed. "Now he is being taken from me, and I have only myself to blame." He was happy, though, that his Bepi would now be a pastor—a true shepherd of souls.

It was on a beautiful Saturday evening in July 1867 that Don Sarto started off on his journey to Salzano, a rich and fertile farming town. When the people heard who their new pastor was to be, they were dissatisfied. "What? the bishop is sending us only an ordinary curate? What can he be thinking of? Such a thing has never happened before. Until now we've always been given a priest who had already been pastor in some other place. After all, we're not a village; we're a town."

When the bishop heard of their discontent, he said only, "I am giving you the curate of Tombolo as parish priest; in this I am doing Salzano a great favor."

And Salzano soon learned that it *was* a great favor. From the first Sunday morning when he so devoutly celebrated Mass and then so simply and appealingly told of his hopes and plans for the parish, he won the hearts of his people.

Don Bepi soon visited all the members of his parish. He shared their thoughts and hopes; their joys, sorrows, and problems became his. The former pastor had seldom been seen in the streets of Salzano; if someone knocked on the rectory door, the priest would open a tiny window and order the visitor to state his purpose in calling while still standing on the street. How different it was when Don Bepi became pastor! The rectory door was always open; a welcoming smile and a comfortable chair awaited every visitor.

He loved the children and was never happier than when he could spare a few moments from his work to romp and play games with them. They would often have races in the narrow streets. And Don Sarto, in his black cassock, would race too. He would run slowly, though, so that he would be the last to reach the goal. The children would laugh delightedly at this, and then Don Giuseppe would say, smiling and wiping his brow, "Isn't it lucky that I became a priest and not a runner?"

Don Giuseppe's sisters came from Riese to keep house for him. They saw to it that everything was clean, and they tried to see that their brother had plenty to eat. But the good souls did not have an easy time of it. For in Salzano, as in Tombolo, it did not take the poor long to discover to whom they could turn for help.

One day, just before dinner time, Don Bepi's sisters came home from a shopping trip. They went to the kitchen to prepare the stew, which they had left on the stove. But there was no pot of stew. Rosine rushed into her brother's study.

"We've been robbed", she cried. "Our stew is gone."

"I'm the thief, Rosine", Don Giuseppe smilingly comforted her. "I gave it to a poor man."

"But what will we eat?"

"Bread and cheese. We will not die of hunger."

Don Bepi gave away everything—clothing, grain, firewood. One day, a priest who was helping in the parish during Lent said to the sacristan:

"This pile of wood has gone down very rapidly. How is it that so much wood is used here?"

"What can you expect?" was the reply. "Here the door is always open."

Don Sarto performed his charitable works simply

by leaving open the doors to his grain cellar and woodshed.

Once, on a cold winter day, Don Sarto's sister noticed that he was not wearing a coat.

"Why haven't you a coat?" she asked.

His reply was simple. "I have no money." He had given away his coat and had no money to buy another. He even pawned his ordination gifts to get money for the poor.

When Don Sarto's sister noticed one day that his socks were in shreds and tried to insist that he buy a pair, he replied, "It isn't necessary. The cassock covers everything."

Don Carlo came one day to visit. Rosine Sarto secretly took him aside and said, "I'm so glad you're here, Don Carlo. Today I met a salesman who is coming to show us some materials, and you must help us."

"Help?" the guest asked in astonishment.

"Yesterday, Don Giuseppe received some money," Rosine explained, "and I'm sure he'll give it all away by tomorrow. He hasn't got a decent shirt to his name. Perhaps if you persuade him, he'll buy himself the material we need to make him a shirt. Won't you try?"

The guest promised to do what he could, and, at the first opportunity, he began to talk about it.

"Nonsense", Don Giuseppe put him off. "That isn't at all necessary. There are people here who need things much more urgently than I do."

So a little trick was planned. When the salesman arrived, Don Carlo took him aside, inspected his samples, and selected a good piece of cloth. Then, as people sometimes do in Italy, he bargained a little about the price. When a fair price had been agreed on, he asked the man to cut the right amount of cloth from the bolt. Only then was Don Giuseppe sent for.

"Here is your material!" his friend told him. "Now pay for it."

The surprised Don Giuseppe could only pull out his wallet and pay. But he was not really happy about it. "Even you are doing things behind my back", he complained to Don Carlo. But Rosine beamed.

"God bless you, Don Carlo", she said as she was bidding good-bye to her guest. "If you hadn't been here today, we would have had neither the money nor the material by tomorrow."

A sense of humor, Don Sarto knew, was necessary in order to mingle with the people as one of their own. Sometimes, though, his humor could result in a bad moment for someone whom the priest knew was not acting as he should. One of his parishioners once asked Don Sarto to write a letter of recommendation for him, stating that he was a good Catholic. The pastor told the man to return on Friday for the letter. Don Sarto was not sure how well the man lived up to his obligations, so he called at his home at noon on Friday. As he reached the door, a strong odor of frying meat wafted from the house. The priest turned and went back to the rectory.

That afternoon, the man called and requested his letter of recommendation.

"Why, this isn't Friday", Don Sarto replied.

"But of course it is", the man cried. "You told me to come back on Friday, and here I am."

"Oh, it couldn't possibly be Friday," the pastor said decisively, "because you had meat for lunch."

The man's crestfallen face told Don Sarto that his point had been well made.

V

# THE "PERPETUUM MOBILE"

A PERPETUAL MOTION machine, or *perpetuum mo-bile*, would be a very remarkable machine—one of the real wonders of the world—if it existed. Such a machine could run day and night without stopping. And the wonderful thing about it is that you wouldn't have to do anything to keep it working. It would run all by itself, without gasoline or any other fuel. The *perpetuum mobile* is a miracle the greatest inventors have tried to produce. But as yet it has not been invented.

The pastor of Salzano was that kind of machine. He was constantly moving and did not allow himself a moment of rest. People wondered where he got the strength to do so much. Soon he was given the nickname *perpetuum mobile.* The name showed the people's appreciation. To them it meant, "When it comes to doing God's work and saving souls, our pastor knows no rest."

Don Sarto began his day's work at five o'clock, when he went to open the door of the church for Mass.

One day a parishioner said to him, "Father, it is your sexton's job to unlock the church door. But the lazy fellow is lying in bed while you do his work. You should see to it that the sexton opens the door each morning."

"Oh, let the poor man sleep in peace", the pastor replied. "Don't you think I'm capable of opening a door? When I am as old as he, I'll be glad to lie in bed too. Then perhaps someone will open the door for me."

Don Sarto worked for his people from dawn till late at night. One of his important tasks was giving religious instruction to the children. He taught them to know and love the truths of their Faith, and he did it by his love of truth and inspired teaching and by balancing scolding with joking. If a youngster was not paying attention, he would suddenly see Don Giuseppe's biretta sailing through the air. "Bring it

back to me", the priest would call out, eyes twinkling, and then the class would remain alert for the
rest of that day.

As he instructed the children, Don Sarto realized
that they were aware of the meaning of the Holy
Eucharist long before they were allowed to receive
Holy Communion for the first time. These eleven-
and twelve-year-old first communicants had really
been ready to receive our Lord from the time they
were seven or eight. And so Don Sarto did something he had always wanted to do. He began to prepare children to receive First Holy Communion at a
much earlier age than usual, even though he would
jokingly say to a misbehaving child in the first communicants' class, "You'll be receiving your First
Holy Communion when your beard is as long as
from here to Rome."

Don Giuseppe was sure that adults too needed
religious instruction. He used to say that if they
really knew all about our Lord's life and really loved
him as they should, they couldn't possibly sin. So he
formed classes for adults too.

One feature of Don Sarto's educational program
was a "dialogue" instruction, which took place in
the church each Sunday evening. Don Giuseppe and
a neighboring priest would stand before the altar and
give an instruction by means of a dialogue, or conversation. This was much more interesting to the
people than a sermon given by one priest. Don

Sarto's parishioners told others about it, and soon crowds were flocking to Salzano from other parishes each Sunday evening.

One pastor went to visit the bishop.

"Your Lordship," he complained, "my church is almost empty on Sunday evening. How can I give a sermon to an empty church? And it's all because of Don Sarto's dialogue instruction. Isn't there something you can do to stop him from attracting such crowds?"

The bishop showed his pleasure at Don Sarto's work by answering in the words of Christ, "Go thou and do in like manner."

When Don Giuseppe had been in Salzano six years, a terrible epidemic of cholera, a serious illness, broke out in the town. The tireless pastor seemed to be everywhere at the same time. He was priest, cook, nurse, and gravedigger.

The pastor would go from house to house, bringing food, medicine, and, above all, the comfort of the sacraments. Day and night he visited the sick, wishing to save his curates from the danger of exposing themselves to infection. He was the staff on whom every member of his parish might lean.

His hands were willing to do any kind of work. "Work", Don Sarto used to say, "is the chief duty of man on this earth. It brings us closer to Christ, who himself, from his youth on, lived a life of poverty and toil."

Once, when he was conducting a burial service, he noticed that there were only three men to carry the coffin. And so, when the prayers had been said and the holy water sprinkled, the country priest joined the pallbearers to carry the body to the grave.

After the cholera epidemic, more than one parishioner declared, "If Don Giuseppe had not been there, I would not be alive today."

The people of Salzano had reason to believe that their pastor was exceptionally favored by God. We know of at least two incidents, occurring at that time, that seem to have miraculous aspects.

One day, Don Giuseppe was walking through the fields just outside Salzano. He heard screams in the distance and saw that a pile of hay on a nearby farm was on fire. The farmer and his family were alarmed because their home was very near the hay mow, and flames were already beginning to lick the house. In a voice filled with faith and confidence, Don Sarto called out, "Don't be afraid. The fire will be put out, and your house will be saved." At that moment, the flames miraculously turned in the opposite direction, leaving the farmhouse untouched.

Another time, the crops of the people of Salzano were being damaged by an insect called the cigar-maker because it caused the leaves of the vines to roll up like cigars. Don Sarto announced to the people that at a certain hour he would ring the church bell. Every member of the parish should then kneel and pray for relief from the destruction the insect was causing. The response to the prayer seemed miraculous, for the insect disappeared and the crops were saved.

Don Sarto's interest in his people extended to their business affairs, their relationships with their employers, and their financial problems. He had long been aware of the position of moneylenders in the community. Many of these men were dishonest and had no concern for the poor who were obliged to borrow. When the poor people of the village needed money to pay the rent or for some other necessity, they had no way of getting it except to borrow from a moneylender. But the fee, or interest, the money-lender charged was so high that it was almost impossible for the borrower to pay back the money, plus the interest. The interest increased as time went on, and finally the poor borrower would be worse off than before he borrowed.

The pastor gathered together a few wealthy members of the parish. They each contributed a sum of money, and this was kept at the rectory as a borrowers' fund for the poor. Money could be borrowed from this fund at a very low rate of interest. The interest charged was just enough to maintain the fund.

This ability of Don Sarto to see the practical, everyday problems of his people was part of his Christ-like charity. And the sanctity of their pastor could not help but bring about a change in the people. The bishop noted this spirit when he visited the parish and wrote in his report: "A wonderful religious spirit flourishes in the parish; there is a happy, united community grouped around a holy, devoted pastor; attendance at the sacraments is consoling; a great number of children are at Communion; there is the greatest regularity in everything concerning the worship of God."

Don Sarto had been pastor at Salzano for nine years, the same length of time he had spent at Tombolo.

In 1876, he received notice that the bishop wished to see him. Don Bepi set out for Treviso, wondering why the bishop could possibly want to see him. Had he neglected his duty? Had he been unworthy of his pastorate?

The bishop received the pastor with kindness and affection. He noticed how thin Don Sarto looked, how worn his cassock was, and how tired he seemed.

"I am very well satisfied with your work, my son", the bishop began. "You are loved by everyone in Salzano. But, my dear Don Sarto, you take too little care of yourself. I have decided to appoint you to another post where you will have a chance to regain some strength."

Don Giuseppe listened in dismay. Must he leave his beloved parish? Would he no longer have his children around him. Would he no longer be a father to the poor people of Salzano?

He begged the bishop to allow him to remain. "I would be satisfied to spend my whole life as pastor of Salzano", he ended humbly.

But all his begging did him no good. "My son, I need you", the bishop replied. "I have been looking for a long time for a spiritual leader who could direct our students while they are on their way to the priesthood. You are just the right man for that. Two hundred small boys and sixty big ones are waiting for you to take care of them."

Then he added with a smile, "I have heard that in Salzano they call you the *perpetuum mobile*. Well, our students will see to it that you get no rest."

With a heavy heart, Don Giuseppe accepted the bishop's wishes and returned to Salzano. The good people of the town were grief-stricken to learn that their pastor would soon be leaving. But Don Sarto's sisters smiled to themselves because they knew that their brother, since he was going to eat and sleep at the seminary, would have regular meals and would no longer be able to give away the food from his table. They packed their belongings to return to Riese, confident that Don Sarto would be well taken care of.

And so Don Giuseppe Sarto soon left for Treviso. All the people of the parish accompanied him. Some rode in fine carriages; others had only farm wagons or poor donkey carts. Some had only bicycles. But, to show their affection for their pastor and to wish him well, they rode with him all the way to the gates of Treviso. Then they sorrowfully turned home.

## VI

## THE CANON AT TREVISO

WHEN DON SARTO went to Treviso to become
spiritual director at the seminary, he accepted
another important position as well. He was named a
canon—that is, he would assist the bishop in the
work of the diocese. The particular work Don Sarto
was to do for the bishop was to be chancellor—to
carry out duties of administering the diocese, to deal
with the problems and questions of parish priests,

and so on. As canon, he received the title of monsignor, so he was now *Monsignor* Sarto.

The new monsignor accepted his double responsibility as the will of God and began his work. One of
his first statements to the seminarians under his
direction was: "I am a poor country pastor who has
been brought here through God's will." He spoke
so beautifully and sincerely about the priestly vocation for which those young men were preparing
themselves that all of them were deeply moved.

Canon Sarto spent a great deal of time with the
seminarians, leading them in prayer and instructing
and counseling them. In addition, he spent six hours
each day in his office in the bishop's residence, han-
dling his work as chancellor. In the evening, when
he returned to his room in the seminary, he brought
with him office work he had not had time to do.
He worked so late that the priest whose room was
next to Monsignor Sarto's sometimes worried about
him.

"Why don't you go to bed?" he called out one
night when Don Giuseppe was still working. "Let
your work go until tomorrow. You know, there's
an old saying—'He who works too long works
badly.'"

"You're right about that", Don Giuseppe
answered with a smile. "That's why I'll give you
some good advice. Go to sleep so you can be fresh
again tomorrow."

Every evening the door to Canon Sarto's room was open to seminarians who wished to talk with him. One evening, a young seminarian came to the spiritual director to ask a favor.

"It is a problem of money, Don Giuseppe. My parents at home are badly in need of 150 *lire*. If only I could borrow enough to help them!"

Don Giuseppe leaned forward. "I'm afraid, my son, that you have knocked on the wrong door. Look, I've got only a few *lire* myself."

And he pulled a shabby purse from a pocket of his cassock. There were four *lire* in it.

The boy looked so discouraged that the priest quickly went on. "But have courage. Stop by again tomorrow. Perhaps by then I'll have something for you."

The next evening the young seminarian again appeared at the door of Monsignor Sarto's room.

"Oh, yes, you've come about the money. Say, do you think I can produce money by magic?" the monsignor began jokingly.

Then, as he looked at the serious face of the boy before him, he continued, "Come in, come in. I have something for you."

He handed over an envelope containing 150 *lire*.

"After you are ordained, you must save your money and pay back the debt. Don't forget, now, because I've had to borrow this money for you."

And, with a clap on the back, Monsignor Sarto sent the happy seminarian back to his room.

Even though Don Giuseppe was as kind as a father to the students, he also had a father's stern resolve that his sons must be all that God intended them to be. He instilled in them the truths that God is the Beginning and the End and that they must detach themselves from the things of the world in order to grow closer to him. Canon Sarto would not tolerate carelessness of any sort in these young men who were to be representatives of Christ's Church.

As chancellor, Canon Sarto was just, careful, and efficient. Some pastors who brought their problems to him said, "Monsignor Sarto is the best chancellor we've ever had."

He carefully managed the business matters of the diocese, but he never forgot that charity and consideration for others were important too. The poverty he had seen in Riese and his concern with the affairs of his people in Salzano had taught him that. He knew it was important that money should be collected and that bookkeeping ledgers should balance, but he knew also that the needs of God's people should come first.

One day, a worried printer came to the bishop's residence. He had come to collect money the diocese owed him for work he had done. It was customary to pay bills on the first of the month, and the printer had been told that he would receive the money then. But he needed it immediately, so he went to see the chancellor.

"I haven't any money myself," Monsignor Sarto said, "but I'll see if I can help you."

He disappeared into the next room. One of Monsignor Sarto's duties as chancellor was to take care of budgeting the money of the diocese among the various departments. There was a cashbox for each sum of money. Now the chancellor was looking in the boxes, taking a little money here and a little there, and replacing the money with a note showing how much had been taken out.

"Here you are", he said as he returned. "I'll collect your money from the bishop at the beginning of the month and replace what I took from the boxes."

As a monsignor, Don Giuseppe was permitted to wear a purple cassock as a mark of distinction. But he always wore the plain black cassock every priest wears.

He was so busy, though, that he rarely had time to go back to Riese to see his family. And when he did go home, it was usually just for a day. His mother often wished that he would stay at home for a visit, so she was overjoyed when she saw him drive up to the door one summer afternoon.

"Dear Bepi, at last you have come for a visit", the little white-haired woman cried. And as soon as she had embraced her son, she asked the question he had known she would ask.

"Now, tell me, how long can you stay?"

"Why, Mama," he replied with a smile, "I shall stay for the rest of the month."

But Mama Sarto knew her son well. She had noticed the twinkle in his eye, so she quickly glanced at the calendar. The date was plain to see—July 31.

"I might have known", sighed the mother, but she could not help laughing as her son patted her shoulder consolingly, threw back his head, and roared at his joke.

All his life, Don Giuseppe Sarto loved a good joke. At mealtime in the seminary, all the priests enjoyed his lively conversation and good humor. And his ability to laugh heartily now and then helped him to work all the harder when the time for joking was over.

So well did Canon Sarto perform his duties that, when the bishop died, he was selected to do the bishop's work until the Pope appointed a new bishop. He did this for nearly a year. But, as always, Don Giuseppe considered himself unworthy.

When a friend wrote to congratulate him on his fiftieth birthday, he answered, "What a poor consolation it is to have become half a hundred years old! I am coming closer and closer to the Day of Reckoning, and I have accomplished so little with which to satisfy God. This sad thought occupies me day and night!"

But, in spite of his desire for a simple, obscure life, those who knew Monsignor Sarto realized that he was destined for great things.

Once, he was visiting Tunisia to carry out some diocesan business. He was with the archbishop of Carthage when a sudden storm arose. The archbishop wrapped his wide red robe about the chancellor to help protect him from the rain.

"Ah, my friend, this red robe is becoming to you", the archbishop remarked. "I see here the symbol of the red that you will wear one day. And the Pope who clothes you in it will be greatly honored because of his choice."

"You are prophesying that such a great event would happen to a poor devil who would never even be able to procure the robe", Don Giuseppe humbly replied.

One day, when Monsignor Sarto had been nine years in Treviso, he was sent for by the bishop.

"Come in, my son", the bishop greeted Don Giuseppe. "Will you come to the chapel with me?" And he led the way to the chapel, where both he and Monsignor Sarto fell on their knees before the Blessed Sacrament. After a few moments, the bishop rose and presented to his chancellor a letter.

"Oh, no," cried Monsignor Sarto, as he read the news of his appointment to be bishop of Mantua, "it cannot be true. I am not worthy of such a position." He bowed his head in grief, but not yet in submission, and prayed.

"Accept; take courage. It is the will of God", the bishop consoled him.

"It is impossible, my Lord. I have not the ability for such a task. I am full of faults and shortcomings. Why should the Holy Father choose me, when there are so many others who are more worthy?"

The bishop's command to his chancellor was to accept, but Monsignor Sarto, in his humility, could not be convinced that he was capable enough and worthy to be named a bishop. He knew that the greater his authority and the higher his position in this world, the more souls there would be under his care. And he was afraid that he was not worthy to be the shepherd of these souls.

So he wrote to the Holy Father protesting his unworthiness and begging him to release him from the appointment. We are told that the reply returned to the monsignor on official Vatican stationery contained just one word, written in the Pope's handwriting: "Obey!"

The future bishop, before going to Rome to be consecrated, returned to Riese, where he was greeted by the joyful ringing of the church bells to welcome the mail carrier's son who had become a bishop of the Church. But Don Giuseppe was weighed down by the thought of the heavy responsibilities of a bishop's office. He tried to tell his mother of his feelings.

"Mama," he said one day, "do you realize what it means to be a bishop—to have in my care the salvation of so many souls? Think of the responsibility! Pray for me, Mama. For if I neglect my duty, I shall lose my soul."

"Bepi," his mother calmed him, "you have managed to do everything well until now. I am sure that you will make a good bishop."

In November 1884, the future Pope Pius X set out for Rome. A few days before he was to be consecrated a bishop, he was scheduled to have an audience with the Holy Father, Pope Leo XIII. And once again, during this audience, Giuseppe Sarto pointed out his own failings and shortcomings. The Pope replied that Monsignor Sarto had already written a letter on the subject, and then he gently added, "But it is Our wish that you go to Mantua."

And what could Giuseppe Sarto do except bow to the will of the Holy Father? "The man who wants to be a good ruler must first learn to obey." He had said that himself in one of his sermons only a short while before. And he wanted above all to be an obedient servant of his Church.

The future bishop of Mantua wrote to his former bishop in Treviso: "What a cross! What a Calvary! I can but say with Jesus, 'Not my will, but thine, be done.'"

And the Holy Father himself said, "If the people of Mantua do not love their new pastor, they are incapable of loving anyone, for Monsignor Sarto is the most lovable of the bishops."

## VII

## BEST BISHOP IN LOMBARDY

THE NEW BISHOP was solemnly consecrated in Rome in November 1884. The cardinal who performed the ceremony was himself a native of Mantua, and he was delighted to have the opportunity to consecrate the new bishop for his home diocese.

Soon after his consecration, Bishop Sarto, accompanied by a priest, happened to be traveling by train. On this train no one recognized him. Riding with Bishop Sarto and the priest in the same compartment were two men who were grumbling loudly about the new bishop of Mantua.

"He's an uncultivated man who knows nothing about how to get along in the world", one of them complained.

"A bishop who was a farm boy!" the other objected. "He won't know how to get along with important people."

Bishop Sarto winked secretly at his companion. That meant, "Keep quiet and don't give me away."

Then he joined the conversation. "You are quite right, gentlemen", he said to his two critics. "I can't understand the Holy Father myself. I can't imagine why he chose that Sarto, of all people, to be a bishop. What do any of us know of him? And until now what has he done that is of any importance? Surely there must have been others better suited to a position of that kind."

Then he told the two men just what the qualities are that a good bishop must have. They listened to him with the greatest attention, for they liked this priest who agreed so wholeheartedly with all their objections. Furthermore, they liked him because he spoke of a bishop's vocation with so much wisdom and eloquence.

As Bishop Sarto neared his station, he left the compartment, saying good-bye to his companions in a most friendly way. When he had left the compartment, the two men turned hastily to the priest who was accompanying him. "Who is that distinguished priest?"

"Gentlemen, that is Bishop Sarto himself", the priest answered, as he prepared to depart also. To himself, however, he thought, I'd like to stay awhile longer and watch those embarrassed faces.

We are told that when the new bishop returned to Riese to visit his family, he showed his mother the beautiful bishop's ring he wore. She looked at the elaborate ring on her son's hand and then held out her own hand with its plain gold wedding band.

"Bepi, your ring is beautiful. But if I were not wearing this ring, you would not be wearing yours." It was true, for had she not been a good Christian wife and mother, her son would probably not have become a priest or a bishop.

Bishop Sarto was so sorry to leave Treviso that he could not bear to say an official farewell. So, early one morning, he left a letter to be read to the students saying good-bye and asking them to pray for "poor Monsignor Sarto". Then he walked alone down the road to where a carriage was waiting for him. No one saw him leave.

The new bishop was to pass through Padua on his way to his new assignment. He wished to offer Mass there at the grave of Saint Anthony and to dedicate himself and his new duties to that great saint.

There is a rule that any priest who comes from another parish must produce a certificate in order to say Mass. This is called a *celebret*.

"Where is your *celebret*?" the priest in charge of

the sacristy demanded of Bishop Sarto, without bothering to look at him.

"I'm sorry," answered the new bishop, "but I don't happen to have it with me." Perhaps he had mislaid the paper when he was packing; perhaps, too, he thought that they would know him in Padua since he had often said Mass there before.

In order to be certain of his facts, the sacristan now began a real cross-examination.

"Where do you come from?"

"From Treviso", was the answer.

"What are you in Treviso?"

"Nothing", said the bishop. And that was true, since he had just left his post there.

"What do you mean, 'nothing'?" the strict sacristan asked. "Aren't you a pastor, a chaplain, or a curate?"

"No."

"That's peculiar. As far as I know, there is a shortage of priests in Treviso. And you are without a position? I can't understand it."

"It's just as I've told you", said the bishop.

"Listen, I know Treviso very well. If you would like me to, I could put in a good word for you there and see to it that you get a position."

"Fine", answered the bishop, for he much preferred to have his old position in Treviso, rather than to be bishop of Mantua. Finally the sacristan allowed the bishop to say Mass. But he watched him very closely; he didn't quite trust this priest who had no assignment! His doubts disappeared, however, as he noted the composure and the piety of this "unemployed" priest from Treviso.

When Mass was over, Bishop Sarto entered his name in the Mass book. "Giuseppe Sarto, Bishop of Mantua" was what the sacristan read that afternoon when, out of curiosity, he looked at the book. "Holy Anthony! Where were my eyes?" he wailed, as he clasped his hands. "A bishop was here, and I treated him in that outrageous way!"

In April, Giuseppe Sarto arrived in Mantua to begin to do the work that would lead Pope Leo XIII to say of him, "Bishop Sarto is the best bishop in all Lombardy."

The new bishop himself, in a letter to his vicar general, said, "Your new bishop, the poorest of all, has but one ambition—to see all the children under his care united into one large, happy family, in the shelter of which their souls will be safe. For the well-being of souls, I shall consider no sacrifice too great, and I have nothing more at heart than your salvation."

The diocese of Mantua was greatly in need of priests. The first year Bishop Sarto was there, only one priest was ordained, although forty were needed. A diocese cannot grow unless there are enough priests for all the parishes, so the bishop, whose work in Treviso had been so closely concerned with young seminarians, resolved to improve the seminary of Mantua. He appealed to the people to support the seminary; he instructed his priests to encourage vocations among the young men of the diocese; he chose the best professors as teachers in the seminary; he closely supervised the classes and taught important courses himself. Within a few years, 147 new priests had been ordained.

Bishop Sarto knew all his priests by name and was a real father to them. He kept in close touch with them and required all new priests to return to the seminary for an examination each year for four years after ordination. If the bishop thought that a seminarian was not fitted for the life of a priest, he did not hesitate to ask him to leave. But he was very kind to these young men and always tried to see that they obtained suitable employment.

"To rule well over something, you must first take a good look at it", Bishop Sarto told himself. He had come to a diocese that he did not know at all. So he made up his mind to visit every single parish. It took the bishop two years to finish the "visitation", as the tour of the parishes was called. He forbade the priests to make any preparations for his visit; he wanted his calls to be as informal as possible. He walked from parish to parish, usually arriving early in the morning. He heard confessions, gave a brief sermon, confirmed the children, and went from house to house visiting the people. He talked with the pastor and each of the curates and even examined the children to see how well they had been taught the catechism.

In one parish the bishop visited, the pastor was often late arriving at church in the morning. He seldom was there in time to hear confessions before Mass, and people who wanted to go to confession were disappointed.

When the bishop arrived early in the morning, he entered the confessional and began to hear confessions. When the pastor finally arrived and saw that someone was in his confessional, he angrily pulled aside the curtain to see who it was. To his horror, he found himself face to face with his bishop. Ashamed, the pastor expected a rebuke, but the bishop only smiled and said not a word. It wasn't necessary; the lazy pastor had learned his lesson.

Bishop Sarto still thought, just as he had when he was in Tombolo, that classes in Christian doctrine were very important—even for adults. So he required each of his pastors to provide this instruction and declared that priests should refuse to give absolution to anyone who prevented others from attending instructions.

He himself loved to teach doctrine, and, if one of his priests was ill or unable to teach the classes, the bishop was willing to walk miles to act as a substitute for him.

One Sunday, Bishop Sarto arrived at a church and

found it empty, with no instruction going on. The bishop told the sacristan to ring the bell to summon the people. When the people had arrived and were seated in church, the bishop ascended the pulpit and began to give the religious instruction. The pastor, who had neglected his duty, hurried to the church, breathless, when he heard the bell ringing. He was horrified to see his bishop in the pulpit.

"Oh, here is your pastor now", the bishop said to the people. "He will continue the instruction."

"Your Excellency," the pastor stammered, "please forgive me. I had to greet some guests."

"If you will let me know the next time you are expecting guests," the bishop replied firmly, "I shall come to take your place in the pulpit."

Because he was a true father to his priests, often Bishop Sarto did not find it necessary to say a word of reproach. Just a look was enough to show his disappointment, and then the priest who had not lived up to the bishop's hopes would resolve to do better and to follow more closely in Christ's footsteps, as his bishop was doing.

Giuseppe Sarto never let his duties as bishop take up so much of his time that he could not keep in touch with the people. Every day he preached from the pulpit, and he took the time to see any parishioner who wished to visit him. We are told that when Pope Pius XI was a young priest, he wished to see the bishop of Mantua.

"I wonder if His Excellency might have a moment to see me", the young priest said to one of the bishop's assistants. "May I make an appointment?"

"An appointment is not necessary", was the reply. "Simply go to the bishop's residence. Go upstairs and knock on the door to the left. But you'd better go early because the place will be crowded later."

The young priest did as he had been told and was cordially greeted by the bishop.

"Have you had breakfast?" the bishop asked.

The priest replied that he had not.

"Come on then. My sisters are out today, but I don't think I've forgotten how to make coffee." And the two future popes sat at the kitchen table in the bishop's residence and drank coffee.

Bishop Sarto's kindness to the poor was known by everyone in the diocese. A wealthy Jew sent the bishop a large contribution to be distributed to the poor. "Bishop Sarto", he said, "will see to it better than anyone else that this money gets into the right hands." And he was right, for Bishop Sarto gave generously to the poor, never inquiring about the religion of the people who came to him and never caring whether or not they were friendly toward him.

Once an uncharitable article, unjustly criticizing the bishop, was printed in a newspaper. The author of the article had not signed his name, but his identity became known.

"Your Excellency," the bishop was advised, "you should not allow this to happen. Report the man so that he may be brought to justice and properly punished."

"Never", Bishop Sarto replied. "What that unhappy man needs is prayer—not punishment."

A short time later, the man lost his fortune, and he and his family were in dire need. He owed a great deal of money and was about to be put into prison. He was saved by money sent to him by the bishop. "Do not mention my name", the bishop told the messenger who delivered the money. "Say that this is a gift from Our Lady of Perpetual Help."

Bishop Sarto's love of the poor was known throughout the diocese. Each year, on Holy Thursday, he brought in the poor of the city and, in imitation of our Lord, knelt and washed their feet.

He sold everything he had of value in order to help the poor. A wealthy woman had given him a beautiful bishop's ring set with a very valuable stone. One day, this wealthy benefactor was visiting the bishop. He noticed that she was looking with satisfaction at the ring on his hand.

"You are right", he said. "It is a beautiful ring. But the stone has long ago been sold and replaced by glass."

Whenever the bishop heard of someone who was in danger or in need, he could not rest until he had done his best to help him. He once heard of a professor, a fallen-away Catholic, who was dying but who refused to see a priest. The bishop went to the home of the professor. When the servant inquired who was calling, he said, "Tell the professor that his friend Sarto wishes to see him."

The sick man was so touched by the humility and kindness of the bishop that he asked to see him and then made his peace with God.

Bishop Sarto retained the same quiet humility he had had as Don Antonio's curate in Tombolo. When Pope Leo XIII celebrated his jubilee in 1888, the bishop went to Rome for the occasion. One morning, he was kneeling in Saint Peter's Basilica when he noticed a canon at the altar ready to celebrate Mass. He was glancing around to try to find his altar boy. The bishop rose from his place and approached the canon.

"Please allow me, Monsignor, to serve your Mass."

"Oh, no, Your Excellency", the canon exclaimed, embarrassed and speechless. "That is the duty of an altar boy, not of a bishop."

"I won't do too badly at it", the bishop replied, eyes twinkling. "You'll see."

"Oh, I know that, Your Excellency. It's just that I don't want you to disturb yourself."

"Let's begin, Monsignor."

The bishop dropped to his knees and served the Mass. Afterward, the monsignor tried to thank him for the honor he had extended.

"The honor", the bishop replied, "is for our common Master whom you were representing at the altar and of whom we are both humble servants."

As bishop, Giuseppe Sarto encouraged frequent reception of Holy Communion, the introduction of the Gregorian chant in all his parishes, and the recitation of the Rosary. In all his actions as bishop, he seemed to be fulfilling his mother's confidence in him: "I am sure that you will make a good bishop."

## VIII

## THE RED HAT

IN THE YEAR 1893, another important letter arrived
from Rome. It announced that the Holy Father
had raised Bishop Sarto to the dignity of a cardinal.
Three days later, the new cardinal was named archbishop of Venice. Bishop Sarto said later that when
he heard the news, he was "anxious, terrified, and
humiliated".

Once again the bishop wrote to the Holy Father asking to be dispensed from this new honor. But he was told that his refusal would cause grave displeasure to the Pope, who was very fond of him. So with tears, Bishop Sarto accepted the appointment as cardinal—"a thing", he wrote, "that must seem incredible to all, for it is most incredible to myself." In Rome, he was greeted by the Holy Father with the words, "We congratulate you, Our beloved son, who have guided so worthily the Church of Mantua—truly a good shepherd of the people!"

On the twelfth of June, Giuseppe Sarto was invested with the magnificent robes of a cardinal. We are told that when Bishop Sarto began to make his preparations to go to Rome for the ceremony, he found that, as might be expected, he did not have enough money to buy the necessary robes. He went to the kitchen to see his sister Rosa, his old cassock on his arm.

"Here, Rosa, let's see if we can dye my old robes. Then I won't have to buy new ones to go to Rome."

"Bepi, you simply can't go to Rome with dyed robes", Rosa moaned, but she prepared the dye because she knew that her brother was determined. But the robes then lost all their color and came out white.

"Well, Rosa, never mind. We're making progress. I'm not even a cardinal yet, and already I have the white robes of the Holy Father."

So the new robes were purchased, and the peasant's son was ready to receive the red hat of a cardinal—a prince of the Church—with the right to participate in the election of the Pope.

Angelo Sarto, the new cardinal's brother—who had traveled so many times with him in the little donkey cart from Riese to Castelfranco—wished to travel with his brother this time too as he set out for Rome.

"I would be very happy to have you come, Angelo", Bishop Sarto replied when Angelo suggested his going along. "But, well, frankly, how much money do you have? You know, it costs quite a lot to get to Rome." The bishop was thinking of his own slim resources and felt that Angelo's could hardly be any better.

"Business hasn't been very good lately, Bepi, but I have 200 *lire* put aside. Will that be enough?"

"Enough! Why, you are a rich man! You could go around the world with that!" The humble, generous bishop was amazed; he himself had seldom had that much money at once.

Later, at Rome, the new cardinal arranged for Angelo to have an audience with the Holy Father. But poor Angelo was so overcome with emotion that he could not even answer the Pope's questions. His brother came to the rescue by asking the Pontiff's blessing for himself and Angelo.

When the news of the bishop's promotion

reached Mantua, there was great rejoicing at the honor he had received, but there was sorrow too, for he was soon to be taken from them and sent to Venice. When the new cardinal returned to Mantua from Rome, his entry into the city was like a triumphal procession. All the bells in the city rang, and the welcomers at the railroad station unharnessed the horses that were to pull the cardinal's coach in order that they might have the honor of drawing it themselves.

Cardinal Sarto returned also to Riese to be greeted by his neighbors and relatives, but particularly to see his aged mother, for he seemed to know that this visit to her would be the last. He rode in triumph along the road from Castelfranco to Riese that he had trod as a barefoot schoolboy, and then he entered the little house of his birth. This was the moment Mama Sarto had always waited for. She received the blessing of her son—a prince of the Church. Now she was ready to leave this world; her work was completed. She died peacefully a few months later.

In Italy at the time, it was necessary for the city government to approve the appointment of its archbishop and give him permission to begin his work. For fifteen months, the city government of Venice delayed accepting the nomination of Cardinal Sarto, who, during this time, continued his work as bishop of Mantua. But when the new archbishop was finally allowed to enter Venice, the rejoicing of the people was greater than ever.

When the cardinal heard of the elaborate preparations being made for his reception, he became upset. "I'd like it best of all if I could arrive in Venice unseen, shut up in a big crate", he grumbled.

Venice—the city of cathedrals and palaces, sunny skies, and canals—prepared a brilliant welcoming. Cardinal Sarto entered the city aboard the king's yacht, escorted by a thousand gondolas along the Grand Canal. The "poor country cardinal", as he called himself, was consoled by the thought, "If I did not know that these honors were meant for Jesus Christ and not for my own poor person, I would feel deeply ashamed."

The Venetians were soon aware of the kind of archbishop they had been given. During his sermon at his first solemn Mass in the cathedral, he said, "It would ill-become me if I did not express my love for you, and my greatest consolation will be to know that you return that love and recognize that your pastor has no other ambition than the defense of the truth and the welfare of his flock."

When the new cardinal archbishop of Venice was ready to make his first visits among his people, he did not go to see the important officials; he called on the poorest and lowliest ones he could find. He went to a humble home where three ill children had not yet been confirmed. The prince of the Church himself confirmed them. Next he went to a nearby hospital to comfort the sick and give them his blessing. Finally, he sought out the jail, to talk with the unfortunate prisoners there.

In addition to his administrative work, the cardinal continued to perform his priestly functions by spending hours in the confessional, teaching catechism, and giving sermons. Once, he had made an appointment to see someone at a church some miles from his residence. A thunderstorm began just as Cardinal Sarto was ready to leave to keep his appointment, but nevertheless he walked the several miles to the church through the downpour.

"Your Eminence, you shouldn't have done that", one of his assistants said later. "You should take better care of your health. It wasn't necessary for you to keep the appointment under those circumstances."

"No one," the cardinal replied, "least of all one of high rank, should keep others waiting. It shows a lack of consideration."

It is said that when the cardinal was addressed as "Your Eminence", he would reply with a smile, "I am the son of a poor family of Riese. There is nothing eminent in that."

He always wore his simple black cassock when he walked the streets of Venice, never wishing to be recognized.

A group of women from Salzano came one day to the cardinal's residence to call on him. But when he appeared, they stood bewildered, not knowing how to address their beloved pastor who was now archbishop of the great city of Venice. The cardinal knew their feelings, and, hands outstretched in welcome, he greeted them, saying, "To you I am always Don Bepi."

Cardinal Sarto received many valuable gifts from the Venetians as tokens of welcome. Among them was an elaborate clock. The cardinal turned it around in his hands, from right to left and from left to right. Then he said with much regret, "It's too bad that my coat of arms is engraved on it. Now I can't even take it to a pawnshop. They would recognize me at once."

The generosity of Cardinal Sarto, as always, knew no bounds. "To get money for his charities," the Venetians said, "he would pawn the cathedral itself." And his sisters, who still cooked and kept house for their Bepi, mourned, "In Venice the poorest of the poor is our cardinal."

He gave everything he had to the poor, sometimes being forced to borrow money to pay his household expenses. He was deeply grieved at the thought of anyone in need. Once, when a parish priest in Mantua requested financial help for his parish, the cardinal was forced to reply: "I am ashamed to answer your request for help with this meager contribution, but I must confess that is all I can do; when I was in Mantua, I was poor, but now I am a beggar."

The enemies of the Church soon discovered that Cardinal Sarto was not a man to be trifled with. When the cardinal was made archbishop of Venice, these people formed a majority in the city, and, as the cardinal made his entrance, he heard cries of derision mingling with the ringing of the church bells. When someone asked him how these mischief-makers should be punished, he answered: "Work! Pray! Elect!"

In 1895, when a new city council was being elected, he not only gave others this advice but followed it himself. He wrote hundreds of letters in order to rally the voters. His slogan was, "Away with the enemies of the people of Saint Mark's!" Thousands flocked courageously to his side and elected a Christian government for the city.

For years, the prince of the Church worked side by side with the government to help the poor and, above all, to provide work and a living wage for everyone. He inspired working men to sanctify their labor by looking upon it as a prayer. Many times he presided over meetings of workers and bitterly opposed injustice on the part of employers. It was Cardinal Sarto who brought back to Venice the lace industry for which it became famous. This industry alone provided employment for thousands. He assisted in the establishment of orphanages and free hospitals to care for the poor.

It is said that the papacy of Giuseppe Sarto was

foretold at least twice during his lifetime. One of his assistants said that, once, when he was accompanying the cardinal to a home where he was to administer confirmation to a sick child, a woman passed them in the street. She was carrying in her arms a three-year-old child.

"Mama," cried the child, when she saw the cardinal, "there goes a Pope."

The assistant called this to the attention of the cardinal, but the humble prince of the Church merely laughed and told his assistant to pay no attention to such nonsense.

Another time, when the cardinal was still bishop of Mantua, a saintly lay brother in a religious house had greeted him by saying, "You will first be cardinal, then archbishop, then Pope."

"There, now, you see how wrong you are?" the bishop had laughed. "If that were to happen at all, I would first be archbishop and then cardinal."

"No", the lay brother insisted. "You will become a cardinal, then an archbishop, and then Pope."

And that was exactly how it happened.

IX

# A POPE IS CHOSEN

B AD NEWS QUICKLY SPREAD throughout the world
on July 20, 1903: "The Holy Father, Leo XIII,
is dead in Rome!" For twenty-five years this Pope
had ruled successfully over the Church of Christ, and
now he was dead at the age of ninety-three.

As soon as the news reached Cardinal Sarto, he
began to make preparations for his journey to
Rome. As a cardinal, he would attend the solemn

rites of mourning for Leo XIII. And immediately after this, the voting to elect the new Pope would begin. The cardinal's sisters anxiously hurried about to help their brother get ready. They packed so many of his belongings that the cardinal told them, "Don't make such a fuss. I'm not going to America, you know. I'll be back in two weeks."

But they sadly shook their heads, perhaps knowing somehow that their brother would never return to Venice. Pope Leo XIII himself had said at his last audience with Cardinal Sarto, "We have a presentiment that our Lord will soon call Us. It may well be that you will be Our successor."

It is a great honor for a city when its archbishop is eligible to take part in a papal election, and the people of Venice took this opportunity to show their affection for their cardinal. He had been with them for the same length of time he had spent in Tombolo, Salzano, Treviso, and Mantua—nine years. He rode through the canal in a gondola amid the waves and cheers of the people along the shore. When he arrived at the train station and saw the crowds surrounding it, the humble prelate thought there must have been an accident, and he hurried out of the gondola to see if he could be some help. But at the sight of him, the throng broke into a resounding roar of enthusiasm, and Cardinal Sarto understood— though he could hardly believe it—that the crowd was there to pay tribute to him.

"Oh, how I hope you may be our next Pope, Your Eminence", a woman said to him as he passed.

"No, no, don't say such a thing", the cardinal replied. "The good God has already shown me too much honor in allowing me to help choose our next Holy Father."

But even at this serious moment, his sense of humor was not lost. "May the Holy Spirit inspire the cardinals to elect you Pope", a bystander said. And the future Pope Pius X, eyes twinkling, answered with a smile, "Give the Holy Spirit more credit than that."

So with his return ticket (for which he had borrowed the money) in his pocket, the cardinal boarded the train. To the tearful Venetians who seemed to sense that they were losing him forever, he promised, "Dead or alive, I shall return to you."

A papal election is one of the more important and impressive events in the world. The Church at such a time looks to the Eternal City of Rome and prays to the Holy Spirit to grant a worthy head. Cardinal Sarto, at his departure, had urged the people of Venice to pray "that the Holy Spirit may descend upon the unworthy College of the Apostles and give the Church a faithful high priest." These were the last words he was to speak in Venice.

From all parts of the world, the princes of the Church gathered in the Vatican. They first attended the funeral of Pope Leo XIII. Cardinal Sarto, ever aware of the temporary nature of the things of the world, noticed that at one point during the ceremony, a guard pushed the Pope's casket with his foot in order to place it in the correct position.

"There, now", Cardinal Sarto whispered to the cardinal next to him. "You see how Popes end up? With a kick!"

A few days later, when Cardinal Sarto had been elected Pope, the same cardinal said to him with a smile, "Don't forget the kick!"

A papal election is called a conclave, which means "a locked room". For when the cardinals come together to vote, most of the Vatican palace is closed off. Each cardinal is assigned a simple room and two attendants to help him. Thus, undisturbed by the world, the cardinals can concentrate on the election, which means so much to the Church of Christ.

The electors gather in the Sistine Chapel at the Vatican twice each day to vote. Sometimes it has taken several weeks for a Pope to be elected, but Pius X was elected on the fourth day.

Sixty-two cardinals had gathered in Rome for the election. There were only two who had been unable to come. A throne with a canopy over it had been arranged for each cardinal in the Sistine Chapel. When a Pope was finally elected, all the canopies would be lowered except the one on the throne of the new Pope.

Many of the cardinals did not know the humble

prelate from Venice. A cardinal from the French city of Bordeaux spoke to him one day in French.

"Your Eminence must be Italian, for I don't know you. Which diocese are you from?"

Cardinal Sarto replied in Latin: "I do not speak French. I am the archbishop of Venice."

"You don't speak French? What a pity! That means you haven't a chance of being elected, for a Pope must be able to speak French."

Cardinal Sarto replied delightedly, "Really? Then I am not eligible? Thank God!"

As the voting began, the eyes of the cardinals were focused chiefly on the famous and saintly Cardinal Rampolla. As secretary of state to Leo XIII, he had worked very closely with the Pope, was highly efficient, and seemed to be the logical choice.

On the first ballot, Cardinal Sarto received five votes. The second time the cardinals voted, his votes were increased to ten. "I think the other cardinals are trying to have some fun at my expense", Cardinal Sarto whispered to his neighbor, for he sincerely believed that the electors would never seriously consider him.

But as the votes for Cardinal Sarto began to increase, the "country cardinal" became frightened. "I am unworthy", he told the other electors. "I am not fit to hold such a high position. Please—I beg of you—do not consider me."

It was this very humility that appealed to the cardinals, for on the third day Cardinal Sarto received even more votes than on the preceding day. Again the future Pope appealed to his colleagues.

"My conscience compels me to tell you that I do not possess the required qualifications. I could not accept. It is your duty to give your votes to someone else."

An American cardinal, who was describing the election later, said, "It was in just this way that we got to know him. In trying to prove to us that he lacked the necessary qualifications to be Pope, he displayed such humility and wisdom that on the next ballot the votes only increased in his favor."

It was clear that on the following day Cardinal Sarto would receive the votes of two-thirds of the electors—the necessary number for election.

Therefore the cardinal deacon—the cardinal who presides at the voting—sent the monsignor who acted as secretary to the conclave to talk with Cardinal Sarto to see if he could be persuaded to accept the papacy. Monsignor Merry del Val found the future Pope kneeling on the floor in the Pauline Chapel, praying, his head in his hands. Once again, with tears in his eyes, Cardinal Sarto refused. "I implore you, Monsignor, ask the cardinal deacon to have mercy on me and forget me."

But the electors joined in persuading Cardinal Sarto to accept.

"Go back to Venice if you wish," Cardinal Ferrari

of Milan told him, "but your conscience will hurt you for the rest of your life."

"The welfare of Christianity requires you to accept", another cardinal urged. "Do you wish to resist the will of God?"

Resist the will of God? No, that was something Giuseppe Sarto had never done. Before the cardinal's eyes loomed the great responsibility of the papacy, but he remembered too the words the Savior had spoken to the first Pope: "I have prayed for you."

On the morning of the fourth of August, when Cardinal Sarto went to the Sistine Chapel, he was hardly recognizable. His step was weary, and on his face there was an expression of unspeakable sorrow. All night he had been praying for strength to face this difficult day.

When the ballots were counted, it was announced that fifty electors had voted for Cardinal Sarto. This was more than the required two-thirds—he had been elected. Pale and in tears, the cardinal sat in his place as the other cardinals rose respectfully and advanced to his throne.

"Do you accept our choice?" the cardinal deacon asked.

A long silence followed. Finally, Cardinal Sarto said, "May the will of God be done."

The answer was not clear, so the question was put to Cardinal Sarto a second time. And this time the man who had been chosen gave the answer that the cardinals longed to hear. "I will accept the papacy, but as a cross. And you, my fathers, must help me to carry it."

This was the moment when Cardinal Sarto became Pope—the representative of Christ on earth, the head of the Church.

"What name will you bear?" This was the next question asked of the new Pope.

"As I shall suffer, I shall take the name of those popes who also suffered. My papal name will be Pius."

Day after day during the conclave, huge crowds had come to stand in Saint Peter's Square in the Vatican to await the outcome of the election. That morning too, thousands of people were standing in the square, looking up to the roof of the Sistine Chapel. Their eyes were focused on the small chimney that has always signaled the election results. For immediately following each balloting, the paper ballots are burned in a small stove. If the vote has been indecisive, damp straw is put into the stove with the ballots. Then the smoke coming from the chimney is dark, and everyone in the square knows at once that a new Pope has not yet been elected. But if the princes of the Church have elected a Pope, the ballots alone are burned in the stove. And then the *Sfumata*—a thin, white wisp of smoke—announces the election to the watchers in the square below.

It was almost noon when the word spread through Rome: "*La Sfumata, la Sfumata* . . . the white smoke!" The news ran through the city like wildfire. "The Pope has been elected!" And at once everyone raced for Saint Peter's Square. For everyone wants to be there when the solemn announcement is made that a new Pope has been chosen. Every Roman naturally considers it a great honor to receive the first blessing of a new Pope.

While the middle window above Saint Peter's was being opened and the balcony decorated, the crowd below jammed tighter and tighter. And always more people came hurrying from every direction. "Who is it?" everyone was asking.

Suddenly there was silence. A cardinal had appeared on the balcony. In a solemn voice, he announced, "We have a Pope once again. It is His Eminence, the Right Reverend Giuseppe Sarto. He has taken the name Pius X."

Even before the cardinal appeared, some of those waiting in Saint Peter's Square had already learned the identity of the new Pope. For a member of the Vatican staff had humorously, but silently, announced it from a window. The word *sarto* in Italian means "tailor", so the staff member held up a pair of scissors and pretended to cut the cloth of the drapery hanging at the window, as a tailor would do. The quick-witted ones standing in Saint Peter's Square could see at once that Cardinal Sarto was the new Pope.

As soon as the announcement had been made, a storm of enthusiasm broke loose. The bells of Saint

Peter's began to peal, and then all the church bells through the Eternal City joined in the general rejoicing. By telephone and telegraph, the news went out to the world: "The Catholic Church has a head once more. He is Pius X, the former archbishop of Venice."

While the bells of the world were still jubilantly pealing, high up in the Vatican palace a man was kneeling in prayer. He was dressed in white, for he had changed his robes as soon as the election was over. Tears were streaming down his cheeks, and his sad eyes looked up at the cross: "My God, what hast thou made of thy unworthy servant?"

In Riese, the little village that had now so suddenly achieved worldwide fame, the church bells were ringing as they had never rung before. They were not silent until the next morning at three o'clock.

One of the Vatican staff members had immediately telephoned the new Pope's sisters in Venice to tell them the news.

"It is my honor to tell you that your brother has been elected Pope", he announced.

"Oh, there most be some mistake. Perhaps you have the wrong number. This is Cardinal Sarto's sister."

"There is no mistake. For an hour you have been the sister of a Pope."

Instead of rejoicing, the sisters of the Pope wept in sympathy for their brother Bepi, who would have to carry such a heavy burden of responsibility and who, they knew, wanted nothing more than to return to his beloved Venice.

After the public announcement had been made from the balcony outside, the people in the square thronged into Saint Peter's Basilica to receive the blessing. When the Pope appeared on the inner balcony, the cry echoed through the basilica, "Long live Pope Pius X."

Then Giuseppe Sarto—successor of Saint Peter and Vicar of Christ—raised his hands in the apostolic blessing. His eyes were weary and sad as he looked out on that vast throng of people—only a tiny handful compared with the numbers all over the world of whom he was now the shepherd. But he knew too that God would inspire and strengthen him to do this work, just as he had always directed him before. And as Pope Pius X looked again at the crowds beneath him—people from all walks and ranks of life—he seemed to see his own farm people of Riese, his simple parishioners of Tombolo and Salzano, his brave young seminarians in Treviso, and all the hard-working, self-sacrificing priests whom he had known in Treviso and Mantua, and, finally, his beloved Venetians. Then not even the awesome thought of his heavy burdens could smother the burning love of Giuseppe Sarto for all men as the warm smile of a father lighted his face.

# X

# THE CORONATION

THE FIRST ACT of Pope Pius X, after he had given
his blessing to the Romans in Saint Peter's, was
to visit the elderly Cardinal Herrero, who was con-
fined to bed by illness. Then he returned to the simple room he had occupied during the conclave to
pray.

That evening, Monsignor Merry del Val came to
the Pope's room to ask him to sign letters to be sent
to heads of governments announcing his election.
The monsignor apologized to the Holy Father for
disturbing him after such a difficult and trying day.

But the Pope, thinking of others as always, lightly dismissed his own exhaustion and said, "But you are tired, too. I noticed that during the conclave you were active all the time."

On his very first day as Pope, the Holy Father sent a telegram to Riese bringing the papal blessing to all his loved ones. "With tears in his eyes," it read, "the Holy Father sends his apostolic blessing to his dear sisters and to the whole family." The very day of the election, the first telegraph office had been opened in Riese, and this telegram from the Pope was the first to be received there.

When the Holy Father retired to his room the first night after his election, a Swiss Guard—a member of the company of soldiers that guards the Pope—stationed himself outside the door. But when the new Pope realized that the guard was preparing to spend the night there, he went to the door and said, "No, no, my good fellow, don't stay here. Go to bed. Then we'll both be able to rest." Then he added, eyes twinkling, "Don't worry, no one will come to steal the Pope."

But Pope Pius reported later, "For the first four nights I never closed my eyes." And it is easy to understand why he could not sleep. He could scarcely believe that so much had happened since he had left Venice a few days before. And now he would never see Venice again; he would remain in the Vatican for the rest of his life. We are told that

some time later, he was seen staring sadly and longingly at a picture of the railway station in Rome,
murmuring "Oh, to get away . . . to get away!"

The first days brought a vast quantity of work.
The solemn papal coronation had already been scheduled for August 9, so invitations had to be sent out as
quickly as possible. But in spite of his pressing work,
Pius X found time to reflect on those about whom
he had always been so concerned—the poor. "Now
all the poor people of Rome are my children", the
newly elected Holy Father announced. The first
amount of money he dispensed from the papal treas-
ury was 100,000 *lire* to be divided among the poor.
But even this large sum of money could not have
been enough to help all Romans who were in need.

The day after his election, the Pope's audiences,
or meetings, began. He had meetings first with the
cardinals who were still at the Vatican. Bishops too
were greeted, and then all the priests of the Eternal
City.

One of the cardinals, Cardinal Merisio, was greatly
moved when he greeted the new Holy Father. He
tried to show his respect by kissing the Pope's slip-
per, but the Holy Father would not allow such a
thing. "My dear Merisio," he finally said, smiling,
"don't make me give your nose a boot."

One of the early audiences given by the Holy
Father was for the diplomatic corps—the ambassadors sent by various countries who wished to be rep-

resented at the Vatican. The ambassadors were very much interested in meeting Pope Pius X because he was so little-known outside of Italy and many of them knew nothing about him.

The Pope's attendants at the Vatican were, in fact, a little uneasy about his first meeting with the ambassadors. Unlike Pope Leo XIII, the farm boy from Riese had had little opportunity in his youth to mingle with distinguished men. But, as Monsignor Merry del Val later reported, the new Pope immediately won over the diplomats, just as he had impressed everyone else who knew him.

"I did not myself take part in the reception," the monsignor recounted, "but I was nearby, working at my desk. A secretary came to me and informed me that the distinguished gentlemen of the diplomatic corps wished to say good-bye to me. I found them in the hall. After the first few words of greeting, there was a pause. I noticed then that there was an air of strangeness about the gentlemen. Their answers were short; all I could find out was that the Holy Father had received them warmly and had spoken a few words to them. Were all of them so silent because some unpleasant incident had occurred? Finally the Prussian ambassador freed me from my fears.

" 'Monsignor,' he asked, 'can you tell us what it is about this man that has such a magnetic effect on everyone?'

"The others immediately agreed and repeated the question to me. Somewhat surprised, I asked the gentlemen if something special had occurred.

" 'No, nothing like that', they answered. 'His Holiness did not talk very long. He simply went around the room, greeting all of us, and then he withdrew. But we were all captivated by his personality.'

"When the diplomats had all left, I asked myself the same question they had asked me: What is it about this man that is so magnetic? What is it that draws us to him? The answer, I think, is clear: he is a saint. He is indeed a man of God."

It was difficult for the new Pope to become accustomed to the traditions of the Vatican. He confided to a friend soon after his election, "You cannot imagine how unpleasant court life is for me. As I walk about surrounded by soldiers, I feel as Jesus must have felt in the Garden of Olives when he was taken prisoner."

Even at mealtime, there were customs to be abided by. For instance, it had been traditional for centuries for the Pope to eat alone. Pius X, however, was determined that he would not be bound unnecessarily by tradition. The day after his election, he noticed that the table in the dining room was set with only one place.

"Please set another place", he said to a servant nearby. "Monsignor Bressan is going to dine here also."

The servant excitedly informed the other servants. They were shocked.

"What? The Holy Father wishes to invite someone to eat with him?"

"Impossible! It just isn't done!"

"Tradition simply cannot be ignored like this. Someone will have to inform the Holy Father of the custom. He is from Venice and probably doesn't understand."

Finally one of the braver servants dared to approach the Pope and tell him that his decision to dine with Monsignor Bressan was contrary to papal tradition.

The Pope could hardly suppress a smile as he said gently, "Well now, are you sure that Saint Peter ate alone?"

"I am not sure about Saint Peter, Your Holiness," the servant replied seriously, "but I do know that our Holy Father Pope Leo XIII ate alone. In fact, every Pope has followed the tradition set centuries ago by Pope Urban VIII."

"Fine, fine", the Holy Father replied calmly. "My glorious predecessor Urban decided that popes should eat alone. He was Pope, so it was his right to decide such a thing. Now, by virtue of the same right, I decide the opposite. I wish Monsignor Bressan to dine with me."

The Pope smiled warmly, and the bewildered servant went off to set the extra place at the table.

As soon as the election of the new Pope had been announced, there was great interest in the history of his life, his background, and his family. Whenever a new head of the Church is named, all the Catholics of the world await news of this man who will be their shepherd. In this case, because Pius X had lived such a quiet, humble life and was so little known outside of the dioceses where he had worked, interest in his history was all the more keen.

The ancestors of the Pope were being traced, and the genealogist who was studying the family approached the Holy Father to show him the results of his work.

"Your Holiness, I have traced your family back to a certain Prosdocimo Sarto, who was born in 1431", he said, proud of his accomplishment. "Here is the chart I have drawn up. Is that correct?"

"Oh, such nonsense!" the humble Giuseppe Sarto exclaimed. "I'm surprised you haven't tried to make me a nobleman. All I know about my ancestors is that I am a descendant of Adam and Eve. That is all we have to know."

On the ninth of August, five days after the election, the solemn coronation of Pope Pius X took place in Saint Peter's Basilica. Except for a canonization ceremony, a papal coronation is the most splendid ritual in the entire liturgy of the Catholic Church. As the Holy Father's throne—the *sedia gestatoria*—was carried into the great cathedral, a crowd of 50,000 was there to acclaim him. When the silver trumpets sounded, the people raised their voices in a roar of greeting. But the Pope instinctively placed his finger on his lips in a command for silence. He later said, "It is not fitting to applaud the servant in the house of his Master."

After the solemn Mass, Pope Pius X was crowned, and as the tiara—the three-tiered crown—was placed upon his head, these words were spoken: "Receive this three-tiered crown, and know that you are now father to kings and princes. As the representative of Christ on earth, it is for you to lead the world in the stead of him to whom all honor is due now and forever more."

The Church, ever fearful lest her children become attached to the things of this world, includes in the liturgy for this occasion—amid all the lavish brilliance of the coronation—a reminder that our stay in the world is only a brief one. Three times the Pope ignited flax in a tiny burner and, as the flax flamed and the smoke disappeared, he heard the words: "Thus passes the glory of the world."

As Giuseppe Sarto—clothed in the elaborate vestments of the Vicar of Christ—raised his hand in the apostolic blessing, his sisters, kneeling in the splendor of Saint Peter's, tearfully remembered the day so many years before when he had first raised his hand in blessing in the little church of Riese.

## XI

# A BLACK CASSOCK BECOMES WHITE

Y EARS BEFORE the coronation of Pius X, when it had been predicted that he would someday become Pope, he replied laughingly, "If I ever become Pope, I will change only my robes." And that was exactly how Giuseppe Sarto did react to his high position. He exchanged his worn black cassock for the white one of the Holy Father, but he was as humble and approachable as he had always been. It is said that—forgetting that he was wearing the white cassock—the Pope often wiped his pen across his sleeve, just as he used to do when he was wearing black.

One day, during the first week following his coronation, a jeweler placed in his hands a very valuable pectoral cross—the cross worn by a Pope around his neck. The man spoke so politely that the Pope was under the impression that the cross was a gift. So he accepted it gratefully. But a few days later, a bill for 6,000 *lire* arrived at the Vatican. That was what the goldsmith was charging for this valuable piece of jewelry. The Holy Father, much alarmed, had the pectoral cross sent back immediately with a note saying that he could not possibly send so much money for a cross.

He had, in fact, pawned his silver bishop's cross, so, when he was proclaimed Pope and was to appear on the balcony of Saint Peter's to give his blessing, he had only a tin cross to wear. "Don't worry", he said to those nearby who were upset about it; "it looks so much like the silver one that no one will notice."

Once, during a public audience, a lady of noble birth held out to the Holy Father a beautiful white silk cap she had made with her own hands.

"Your Holiness," she asked, "would you do me the honor of accepting this cap which I have made?"

The Pope smiled kindly and accepted the gift.

The lady, encouraged by the Pope's acceptance, found the courage to speak again.

"Most Holy Father, would you not consent to give me in exchange, as a memento of this meeting, the cap you are now wearing?"

The Pope removed from his head the coarse, white woolen cap he was wearing, so poor in quality compared with the fine silk one he had just accepted.

"When you bring me one just like this," he said, indicating his woolen cap, "I shall consent to the exchange."

As a boy, Giuseppe Sarto had been poor. He was poor as a bishop and as a cardinal. And Pius X wished to remain poor, too. He still used his old spectacles and his shabby wallet, which was just as empty now as it had always been. He still carried his worn watch, made of nickel and hung on a leather strap. During an audience, a wealthy man who was standing near the Holy Father noticed the condition of the watch. He immediately drew out his own gold watch, set with jewels, and offered it to the Holy Father. But the Pope graciously declined the gift.

"This watch", he said, "was given to me by my mother when I was still in school, and she worked hard to get it for me. It is one of my most precious possessions; I would never part with it." Then he added, smiling, "The watch has repaid me for my faithfulness, too. It has always worked perfectly."

His brothers and sisters soon discovered that as Pope, Giuseppe Sarto intended to remain the same man he had been before. When they appeared at the Vatican for their first visit to their distinguished brother, they were not certain how they should behave. A visit to the Holy Father, the head of the Church! How should one behave on such an occasion, even if the Pope is one's own brother? They decided to follow the custom of kneeling in the presence of the Holy Father. But Pius X, deeply moved, raised up his sisters and brothers and embraced them. "What are you thinking of?" he said. "I am still your Bepi." And they all sat down and chatted, just as they always had in the little house in Riese.

That same week a high Vatican official came to see the Holy Father to ask him what titles or honors he would like to bestow on his sisters, for in former days it was customary for a new Pope to raise his brothers and sisters to the ranks of the nobility.

"Titles?" the Pope asked in astonishment.

He thought for a moment. "Sisters of the Pope!" was the answer the smiling Pius X at last gave to the official, who was standing before him, awaiting his decision. The official started to object.

"It is an ancient custom, Your Holiness. You understand, do you not?"

"Sisters of the Pope!" the Holy Father said again, speaking this time with a little more emphasis. But the official could not believe that the Holy Father would not bestow a noble title upon his sisters.

He tried for the third time. "Your Holiness will decide whether it is more fitting to give them the rank of duchess or princess."

For the third time the Holy Father repeated his wish. "Sisters of the Pope!" he said. "That is a title that no one but they, in all the world, can enjoy. What better title can I bestow on the sisters who have done so much for me? And now, let us not have another word on this subject. My relatives will remain what they have always been—the Sarto family of Riese."

The Holy Father was very fond of his nephew, who was a priest in a country parish. Everyone was anxious to see what the new Pope would do for this favorite nephew. Surely he would make him a bishop in one of the large cities! But the Pope made no mention of his nephew when he announced appointments to various positions. Finally a friend, thinking that perhaps the Pope had forgotten to promote his nephew, said to him one day: "I am going to Possagno and will see your nephew, Your Holiness. Would you like me to give him a message from you?"

"Yes, indeed", the Pope replied. "Please give him my best wishes for good health and my blessing."

And the Pope's nephew remained a country pastor until after his uncle's death.

The Holy Father, whenever he could, simplified the rigid regulations of the Vatican so that he could have more privacy and live, as much as possible, as he had done in Venice. Many years earlier, a large part of Italy had been controlled by the Pope, so he was really a political ruler, just like the kings and heads of government in other countries. Because the Holy Father, even now, is given equal rank with these rulers and because of his exalted position as Vicar of Christ, he is attended by numerous Vatican Swiss Guards whenever making an official appearance. Pope Pius X, however, was not happy about this.

"I can never step out of my room", he once exclaimed, "without having four guards present arms and follow me!"

Soon the Pope issued a decree that his bodyguard should be reduced to half the usual number. Once, in fact, the Holy Father succeeded in slipping out of his room unnoticed. He found his way into the Vatican gardens through secret passages, happily seeking the most out-of-the-way paths so that, for once, he could be alone and undisturbed. He laughed heartily afterward when he learned that the guards had been searching desperately for him. "They searched for me as if I were the most notorious criminal", he used to say later.

One day a French bishop had an audience with the Holy Father. As is customary on such a visit, the bishop knelt at the feet of the Holy Father. But Pius X raised him up immediately, saying, "It is not fitting for you to kneel before me, for I am only the very least of Christ's priests."

The Pope never forgot his years as a young parish priest, and he fondly recalled the good people he had known at that time. A very touching meeting once took place at the Vatican between the Holy Father and the elderly Vincent, who had been sacristan at Tombolo when the Pope was assistant to Don Antonio. Vincent, who did not tell anyone that he had once known the Holy Father, was one of a large group of pilgrims who had been granted an audience. It happened that just before the audience, the Pope had had a serious talk with a bishop, and he was so preoccupied with what had happened that he scarcely noticed the faces of the kneeling pilgrims. As the Pope passed him, Vincent was so overcome at seeing "Don Giuseppe" that he reached out for the hand of the Pontiff, kissed his ring, and then burst into tears.

"Why, what is it, my son?" the Holy Father asked kindly, as he stopped and looked at the sacristan. "Vincent," he cried then, as he recognized his old friend, "is it really you?"

"Yes, Holy Father, it is I", Vincent replied, overjoyed at this recognition. Then, not knowing what to say next, the sacristan asked, "How do you feel, Holy Father?"

The Pontiff smiled and replied, "Well, I feel . . . like a Pope."

Then the Holy Father asked for all the news of Vincent's family and the other people of Tombolo, and the elderly sacristan returned to his home town to cherish all his life and to pass on to his children the memory of that unforgettable meeting.

Pope Pius X—always sensitive to the problems of his cardinals, bishops, and priests—was just as sensitive to the problems of the employees of the Vatican. One of the elevator operators—whom the Pope teasingly called "Towhead" because of his blond hair—was very unhappy because of financial difficulties at home. The Pope heard of the boy's problem, but he said nothing about it. The next time he got off the elevator, he turned back as if he had forgotten something. Then, when no one could see him, he pressed a hundred *lire* into the boy's hand, whispering, "Now, Towhead, try to be happy again!"

The humility of the Pope was so great that when the Venetians wished to place in their cathedral a stone engraved with a tribute to their former archbishop, the Pope forbade it. The canons of Treviso wished also to place a commemorative stone in the cathedral. The Pope, however, wrote to them: "If the reverend canons of the Cathedral of Treviso are desirous of pleasing the Holy Father, they remember him in their Masses and prayers and abandon the thought of 'stoning' him."

The Pope humbly accepted advice and suggestions, even giving his secretaries permission to correct his letters, if they felt it necessary. He read his speeches to his secretaries and was glad to receive their suggestions for improvement. "Those are to be pitied", he once wrote, "who, obstinately clinging to their own ideas, find opposition at every step, because they lack the tact which humility teaches."

When a certain monsignor visited the Pope in his office early one morning, he noticed that the Holy Father had already written about a dozen letters.

"Your Holiness," he commented, "you should not tax your strength. Could not your secretaries write some of those letters?"

"Oh, I don't mind", the Pope replied. "I like to save them as much work as possible."

At the end of a conversation, the Holy Father always requested the prayers of his visitor. For, as he wrote later, "if the favorites of the Lord do not pray that I shall be able to carry the cross that has been placed upon my shoulders, how can I hope to climb Mount Calvary?"

## XII

## FATHER TO ALL THE WORLD

WHEN, ON AUGUST 4, the Sarto sisters first heard that their brother had been made Pope, one of them cried, "The poor man! Now you'll see . . . he'll have to help the poor all over the world." She knew so well her brother's sympathetic heart.

All the news of the world—good and bad—is reported at once to the Holy Father in Rome. But in the time of Pope Pius X, just as today, there was more bad news than good. There were more reports of sickness, disaster, and affliction than of peace, happiness, and well-being.

The Pope's fatherly heart went out to everyone in need. In 1908, he was grief-stricken by reports of a terrible earthquake in southern Italy. About 100,000 people were killed, and many others were injured or left homeless. When the tragic news reached the Pope, he exclaimed at once, "We must help immediately!"

The Holy Father issued a call to the Catholics of the world to help the victims of the earthquake. They responded so generously that the Pope was able to arrange for the construction of 218 churches, 158 homes, 26 schools, and 20 centers for the care of children. He spared no effort to seek out the poor and orphaned, reunite separated families, greet the injured who were sent to Rome, and encourage all those who were helping to lighten the burden of the suffering.

The Pope arranged for 575 orphaned children to be brought to Rome and placed in institutions where they would be well cared for. "They will be my children now", he said. He never forgot these children, and he generously provided for all their needs and for their education.

Many people, knowing how the Pope suffered when he did not have the money to help those in need, brought him valuable gifts. And the Catholics of the world gave generously to the annual "Peter's

Pence" collection, for everyone knew that the Holy
Father's greatest joy was to receive money he could
donate to the poor.

Once, when the Pope was leaving his apartment
with a companion to stroll in the Vatican gardens, he
was reminded that he had not locked his door.

"There is no reason to lock my door," he replied,
"because there is nothing to steal. Today I gave away
the last penny I had."

It is easy to love and be generous when one is
loved in return. But only a saintly father can love
when he is hated and do good when he is repaid
only with thanklessness. One day, just before the
Holy Father was to enter a room to greet a group of
pilgrims, one of his attendants came to tell him that
among the visitors was a man from Venice who had
been very unpleasant and hostile to the Pope when
he had been archbishop of Venice.

"Fine", said the Holy Father. "Please go to my
office and bring the most beautiful gold rosary you
can find." The Pope greeted all the pilgrims kindly,
but when he came to the Venetian he stopped,
extended his hand, and said, "I am so glad to see
you. How is your mother? Please give her this rosary
and bring to all your family the apostolic blessing."
With tears in his eyes, the man later declared that the
Pope was a saint.

The Pope loved every person so deeply that he
could win over even those who hated him. "If the

Savior were once more to walk the earth," someone
once said, "I think he would look like Pius X."

When a bishop from South Africa arrived in
Rome to solicit funds for his missionary work, he
visited the Pope and told him of his problems.

"Never mind, Monsignor", the Holy Father consoled him. "Have confidence, and help will come.
But for now, take this." He placed in the bishop's
hand a large amount of money.

"Oh, Your Holiness," the bishop gasped, "I would
not dare take such a large amount as this."

"Who is Pope—you or I?" the generous Holy
Father teasingly replied. "All that bishops have to do
is obey."

There is something special about people who do
good. Their hands are never empty, and they never
seem to be poor. There seems to be something of
God's wealth about them. So it was with Pius X.
The more he gave away, the more he received.

Once, a Portuguese bishop was visiting the Holy
Father. He had come as a representative of all the
bishops of Portugal. The Church there was being
persecuted, and they were in great need.

The Pope was moved by this description of tragedy and said, "I will do all I can to help. How much
do you need?"

"At least a million *lire*", was the reply.

"I haven't got that much, but come back tomorrow. I will see what I can do."

The next morning the million *lire* had been collected. Just as the Pope was ready to go into the next room to give it to the Portuguese bishop, a messenger came to say that a gentleman had requested an audience with the Pope.

"Please take this to the bishop from Portugal", the Pope said to one of his companions. "Meanwhile, I shall receive the other gentleman."

When the companion returned, the Holy Father showed him a check for a million *lire*.

"God has not forsaken us", he said. "A million went out by that door and, almost at the same moment, it came back to us through this door."

When Pius X had been bishop of Mantua, his generosity was known to many. One poor man, Pietro Lazze, was often helped financially by the bishop, who treated him with all the kindness of a father. When Giuseppe Sarto was named a cardinal, Pietro came to thank him for all his goodness.

"You see, Your Eminence," he said, smiling, "mankind is divided into two classes—the lucky and the unlucky. Your Eminence belongs to the first group; I am a member of the second. Now you are a cardinal, and soon they will make you Pope."

"You're a bad prophet, Pietro", the cardinal had laughingly replied. "But if it should turn out that you are right, I'll make you captain of my Guard of Honor when I'm Pope. Then you too will be one of the lucky ones."

Pietro never forgot this promise. Whenever he wrote the cardinal in Venice to ask for charity, he always signed the letter: "Pietro Lazze, captain of the Guard of Honor (hopefully)".

Naturally, he recalled the promise when his distinguished patron ascended the papal throne. But when he wrote to the Pope to offer his best wishes, he closed the letter with the words: "I absolve Your Holiness from your promise. In any case, I would not feel comfortable in the job." The letter was signed: "Pietro Lazze, captain of the Guard of Honor (retired)".

The Holy Father replied with a warm letter in his own handwriting, as well as with a generous gift. Pietro proudly showed the letter to his friends in Mantua and kept it as a memento of the kindness and humility of the Pope.

One day, the Holy Father was visited by the cardinal of Bordeaux, France. This was the cardinal who had warned Pius X at the time of the conclave that he could not be elected Pope because he did not speak French. Now the cardinal had come to pay his respects to his Holy Father, and many a spectator wondered how he felt as he recalled his words and the unexpected events that had followed.

The Pope, speaking in correct and fluent French, warmly greeted the cardinal. Then, fearful lest his guest be uneasy at the thought of his hasty words some time before, the Pope remarked humbly, "I took lessons in French, you see, soon after the election, as a result of your very good suggestion."

Pope Pius X, as father to the world, recognized as one of his first duties a father's obligation to teach his children. Just as he had always demanded—as priest, bishop, and cardinal—that Christian doctrine be taught to the people, adults as well as children, Giuseppe Sarto as Pope sent out to all the world the same strong message. He himself loved to stand on the balcony of Saint Peter's Basilica and preach to the people of Rome. He would explain the gospel of the Sunday with all the sincerity and simplicity that had endeared him to the farmers of Tombolo and Salzano.

Pius X, just like every good father, sometimes found it necessary to scold his children. But he did so only with a heavy heart and with a sympathetic understanding of the weakness of human nature. Once, when he was obliged to admonish someone for neglecting his duty, he was so concerned with the problem that he could not sleep the night before. Weeping, he asked Cardinal Merry del Val to pray that our Lord would inspire him to say the right words and that the man would see that he had been wrong. Later, overjoyed, he told the cardinal that, although he had been just and had admonished the man as severely as he deserved, all was well and the shirker had repented. "Now we must do all we can to help him", the Holy Father resolved.

The Pope was full of charity and forgiveness when

an injury had been committed against him. "It is not for us to judge, but the Lord", he would say.

Even though he was always ready to do battle in order to prevent the spread of error, he was determined that every kindness should be shown his enemies. "Since we are forced to fight for the truth," he said, "let us embrace with love the enemies of the truth and commend them to divine mercy."

Before making a serious decision, the Pope prayed long and fervently before the crucifix. He had accepted the papacy as a cross, and so he continually turned to the crucified Savior for the strength and inspiration to carry it. When he had been asked, after his election, what his policy as Pope would be, he had turned to the crucifix hanging over his desk and said, "This alone is my policy."

After prayer and careful reflection on a problem, the Holy Father would make his decision. And then nothing could sway him. "The new Pope is a man of iron", an old Venetian had remarked when Cardinal Sarto had been elected.

A newly appointed bishop once approached the Holy Father and asked to be excused from such a terrible responsibility. He gave several weak reasons why he should not be appointed. The Pope probably remembered the hesitation he himself had felt at the time of his own appointment, but he knew too that firmness was necessary in carrying out the will of God. "Monsignor, I am the Pope, and it is for you to do the will of the Pope", he stated, and the matter was closed.

"There was no shade of weakness in him", Cardinal Merry del Val wrote. "He had the inflexible firmness of a ruler fully convinced of the responsibilities his high office imposed on him, and he was determined to fulfill them, cost what it might."

The Russian ambassador to the Vatican once discovered the firmness of the Pope. Shortly before his death, Pius X granted this ambassador an audience. But he received him sternly, without a trace of a smile on his face. Full of majesty, he turned to his visitor. "I cannot accept good wishes from the representative of a power that fails to keep the promises it makes. Until now Russia has not kept a single one of the promises she made to the Catholics of Russia."

The ambassador had not expected such a greeting, and he was frightened. "Holy Father," he stammered, "that is not true!"

The Holy Father rose from his throne and, with a gesture that betrayed deep indignation, cried, "I will repeat what I have said: not a single promise has been kept! And you dare to say that I lie, Mr. Ambassador! I must ask you to leave this room."

As pale as death, the ambassador stumbled out the door.

So with firmness and mercy, Pope Pius X carried on his work—a worthy successor to Peter, of whom it was said, "Upon this *rock* I will build my Church."

## XIII

## AN ARDENT FIRE

THERE IS AN OLD papal prophecy, the prophecy of Malachy. In it every future Pope is characterized in one small sentence. No one knows if these predictions are authentic, but one cannot help noticing how aptly the work of each Pope is described, often in only two or three words. Of Pope Pius X the prophecy says: "He will be an *ignis ardens*, an ardent fire."

And how well that description fits him. An ardent fire! For the restless *perpetuum mobile* of former days had become the serene, clear-seeing man who inaugurated a wonderful program: to renew all things in Christ. This had been Giuseppe Sarto's motto as bishop and cardinal, and in his first message, or encyclical, he made it clear that this would also be his aim as Pope. To bring all men to the feet of Christ, to instill in them such a strong love that their lives would be centered in Christ—that was the glorious aim of the papacy of Pius X.

Again and again, with his warm and loving heart, the Pope sought to fire a cold world with the love of Christ. Then a great thought came to him. Did a small light not burn before the tabernacle in order to show that here was the home of Love Everlasting? Was it not possible that Christ, who had in his lifetime inspired the apostles, might once more awaken and fire new apostles? Could the small, white Host not bring new strength to the Christians of the twentieth century also?

Pope Pius X turned these thoughts over and over in his mind. And so he became "the Communion Pope", the Pope who was to open wide the tabernacles of the world and invite all Catholics to go to Holy Communion frequently—even every day.

At that time, many people felt only the very holy could receive Holy Communion frequently. Most people received only once a month, or in some cases less often than that. Even Giuseppe Sarto, when he was a student in the seminary preparing for the priesthood, was allowed to go to Holy Communion only once or twice a week. How often he must have looked longingly at the tabernacle and envied the priest who had the privilege of receiving Christ each day.

Pope Pius X pointed out that in the early days of the Church, all those who attended Mass, if they were in the state of grace, received Holy Communion. The Church had always urged the faithful to receive the Blessed Sacrament frequently, but many people, aware of their unworthiness, hesitated to approach the altar more often than once a month. None of us is ever worthy to receive our Lord, the Holy Father said, so receiving him infrequently will not make us any more worthy. Besides, our souls need the nourishment and strength of the Divine Bread, he continued, so we should approach the altar as often as possible.

"Holy Communion is the shortest and surest way to heaven", the Pope claimed. "It is easy to go to the banquet of the Lord, for there we can taste the joys of paradise in advance."

Pope Pius X knew that only through Holy Communion could the souls of the faithful be nourished and strengthened. But he knew, too, that we can love only what we know. If people were ignorant of God and did not know of his love for them, they could not love him in return. The catechism, Pius X said, would provide this knowledge of God; it was like a plow that prepared the soul to receive the seeds of grace. The Holy Father longed to walk among the children as he had in Salzano and Venice, teaching them the catechism as they strolled along. But now—a "prisoner of the Vatican"—he contented himself with preaching to the people each Sunday from the balcony.

"More people hate Christ, despise the Church, and ignore the Gospel because of ignorance than because of malice", the Pope declared. "These unfortunate people blaspheme a God whom they have never been taught to love." To make sure that his flock learned about God so that they could then love him, the shepherd laid down strong regulations for the teaching of the catechism. All priests were to teach their people and to urge their parishioners also to take part in this noble work of sowing in young minds the seeds of sanctity.

Pope Pius X concerned himself immediately with priests and their training. "The priest is the light of the world, the salt of the earth", he said. "How much a priest, even the lowliest, can do if he be holy." And the Holy Father wished to see to it that priests were educated to be truly holy. He issued advice and instructions that are still followed in training priests to be "the light of the world".

The Holy Father, as Bishop of Rome, has special

charge of the Eternal City. So, soon after his coronation, Pius X decreed that a pastoral visitation should
take place in the city. Statistics were gathered in
every parish, and as a result of the visitation, parish
boundaries were revised, new parishes were established, and the entire physical structure of the
Church in the city of Rome was reorganized and
vastly improved.

Another accomplishment of Pope Pius X was his
work in the field of canon law. Until his time, the
Church had never had a complete collection of all
her decrees and documents on discipline. They were
scattered throughout many volumes, and some had
been changed or were no longer in effect. As bishop
and cardinal, the Holy Father had had occasion to
consult books on Church law, and he had often
thought that these laws should be gathered into one
book for the benefit of everyone.

Just a few months after his election to the throne
of Peter, Pius X ordered that this work of codifying
the laws of the Church should be started. "We has-
ten this measure," he said at the time, "for advanced
age makes us fear that We will not see its completion." The Holy Father lived eleven more years, and
most of the work of codification was completed
before his death. But he did not see its completion.

When his successor, Pope Benedict XV, published
the *Code of Canon Law*, he said, "Divine Providence
has arranged that the honor of bestowing this tre-

mendous service on the Church goes to Our predecessor, Pius X, of happy memory. . . . While it was
not granted to him to see its completion, the honor
of the work is his alone."

The year after he became Pope, Pius X—in honor
of the fiftieth anniversary of the proclamation of the
dogma of the Immaculate Conception—issued his
encyclical on this dogma. By dedicating to the
Blessed Mother the second encyclical of his reign, he
effectively placed his work as Pope under her protec-
tion. The Holy Father had always been devoted to
Mary. He was consecrated bishop of Mantua on one
of her feast days, and because of this he felt that she
would protect him and inspire him in his work
there. He often led processions of seminarians to
Mary's shrines where he recited the Rosary and
expressed to them his love for Christ's Mother.

When he became Pope, the Holy Father's devotion to Mary was as fervent as ever. Wherever he
was, he never failed to kneel and recite the Angelus
when the bells tolled, and he delighted in visiting the
shrine to Our Lady of Lourdes in the Vatican gardens. In his encyclical in honor of the Immaculate
Conception, he proclaimed that all the world should
have devotion to Our Lady of Lourdes, who had
identified herself as the Immaculate Conception.

The Sartos—like so many Italian families—loved
music, and Giuseppe could read any score at sight.
He sang well and had such a great love for music

that he felt it should have an important part in the worship of God. But Church music—since it was to be a prayer—must be as perfect as possible, and Giuseppe Sarto had insisted, from his days as assistant at Tombolo, that the people learn to sing the Mass. "I want my people to pray in beauty", he said when he became Pope. And throughout his reign, he encouraged the growth of appropriate Church music, even founding a School of Sacred Music.

Throughout the years of his reign as Pope, Giuseppe Sarto remained in his heart the quiet, country curate—the gentle, beloved father of men—but the solid accomplishments he left behind remind us that he was an *ignis ardens* as well.

## XIV

## THE CHILDREN'S POPE

THE EIGHTH OF AUGUST should be celebrated by all Catholic children of the world as a great feast day because on that day Pope Pius X gave them the most wonderful gift on earth—the Savior in the Host. The Holy Father decreed in 1910 that, as soon as children had reached an age when they were capable of understanding what they were doing, they should be allowed to come to the altar rail.

Bepi Sarto himself had not received his First Holy Communion until he was eleven years old, although he had often begged the pastor, Don Tito, to allow him to receive earlier. But always the answer was the same. "You must be older and wiser, Bepi, before you can receive our Lord."

"But, Don Tito, I know that our Lord is truly present in the Blessed Sacrament. What else must I know?"

"You cannot receive Holy Communion so young, Bepi", Don Tito would reply. Then he would wink at the earnest little lad and say, "Some day, Bepi, when you are Pope, you can grant permission to all the children of the world to receive Holy Communion at an early age."

"This ruling must be changed!" Pius X said sixty years later. "The child loves Jesus and wants to possess him. Why should we not give him to children sooner?"

Some people said that children should not be allowed to receive because they were so thoughtless, but the Pope answered, "Thoughtlessness is no obstacle to Holy Communion. Children *are* thoughtless, but they are at the same time good and loving. Because they want so much to love Jesus, we must give them the Savior in time so that he can nourish them."

What a sensation it created when the Holy Father—the friend of all children—spoke like this. Even some bishops and priests did not understand.

"But, Holy Father," they objected, "what will happen if young children of six and seven are allowed to go to Holy Communion? They can't possibly understand this great secret of the Faith."

"Do you understand it yourselves?" the Holy Father asked them. And they had to admit that they could not.

But still they tried to impress the Holy Father with their ideas. "Holy Communion is so sacred", they objected, "that before receiving, one should be more mature than a small child."

"If children are able to love the Savior, then they are also able to take him to their hearts", the Pope maintained. "When they can understand that the Host is not ordinary bread, then they know enough. Then they know everything they need to know to receive Holy Communion."

The Pope was asked, "Wouldn't it be more sensible to give Communion to children only when they are getting ready to leave school and face life—when they are twelve or fourteen?"

"On the contrary, it may be too late then. It is much better to let children receive Jesus while their hearts are still free from guilt. Jesus loves the child so dearly in his christening innocence. The sooner he enters a child's heart, the sooner will the devil lose his influence."

After the Holy Father had issued his decree, he had the children of Rome come in groups to see him in the Vatican. There he would instruct them himself. Their eyes shone as the Pope spoke to them about Jesus. What joy they felt when finally they were allowed to receive their First Holy Communion from his own hands!

The Holy Father would walk among the children, talking to them and asking them questions. He loved to hear their innocent answers. The Pope's chamberlain—who accompanied him during audiences and whose duty it was to see that visitors addressed the Pope correctly and behaved according to the formal Vatican rules—was often shocked at the informal way in which the children spoke with the Holy Father. Often they forgot the rules and would answer, "Yes, Pope." But Pius X, who knew how to evaluate the rules properly, loved their unspoiled innocence. One little boy, so overcome at the sight of the kind face of the beloved, white-clothed figure, once whispered, "Yes, Jesus."

One day a lady brought her little son with her to visit the Holy Father. While his mother talked with Pius X, the child stayed obediently in a nearby alcove. When the audience was over, he was called and told to say good-bye to the Holy Father. Lovingly and kindly, the Pope held the small hands of the child tight inside his own while the little boy looked up at him with trustful eyes.

"How old is your child?" the Holy Father asked the mother.

"He is just four," she said, "and in two years I hope he will make his First Holy Communion."

Thoughtfully the Pope looked down into the child's eyes and asked, "What does one receive in Holy Communion?"

"Jesus Christ", answered the child at once.

"Who is Jesus Christ?" the Holy Father continued.

"He is the dear God", was the answer.

Without knowing it, the child had taken an examination and passed it with flying colors. The Holy Father turned to the surprised mother.

"Bring your child to my Holy Mass tomorrow morning", he said. "I myself will give him his First Holy Communion."

Children all over the world felt so close to this gentle friend that they often wrote him letters. When they told him of their sorrows, he was troubled; when they told him of their joys, he was happy. Pius X kept all these letters in a special place in his desk and often, when he was worried and concerned about some important problem, he would pick up one of these letters written with love and innocence, and his mind would be eased.

One day a French boy named François decided to write to the Holy Father. He was soon going to make his First Holy Communion—on Easter Sunday—and he was very happy about it, but he was troubled too. His father had not been attending Mass and receiving the sacraments, and when François had asked him to receive Holy Communion with himself and his mother on Easter, the father had laughed scornfully and refused. François decided to ask the Holy Father to write to his father. Surely he would persuade him to return to the Church.

"Dear Holy Father", he wrote. "My name is François, and I am going to receive my First Holy Communion on Easter Sunday. I am very happy, but I also have a big worry. Last night my Papa told my Mother that he would not receive Holy Communion with us that day. He said (I hardly dare write it, Holy Father!), 'That's nonsense!'

"Please write my Papa, dear Holy Father, that he should receive Holy Communion with Mother and me. Then he'll surely do it."

"What do you think", the mother said to her husband when he came home that night. "François has written to the Pope."

"To the Pope? What's the matter with that boy? Let me see the letter. We can't let foolishness like this go out in the mail without reading it first."

"What does it say?" his wife asked after he had read the letter.

"Nothing interesting", her husband replied, and he put the letter in his pocket, resolving not to mail it.

The days went by, and François was grief-stricken because no reply had come from the Pope. The day before Easter, he reminded his father that his letter had not been answered. "Do you think the Pope forgot, Papa?"

"Wait till tomorrow, son. You'll surely have an answer then."

On Easter Sunday, when François saw his parents walk together to the altar rail, he knew that his letter had indeed been answered—even though it was still in his father's coat pocket.

Some time later, the parish priest from the town where François lived was having an audience with Pope Pius X. He told the Pope of the incident, and the Holy Father was deeply touched by the faith of the little boy and the result it had brought about.

When children wrote to the Pope, they talked to him as to a father. "Dear Holy Father," one of them wrote, "I am nine years old, and I've been able to receive Holy Communion for some time now. I know I have you to thank for that. I don't know how to tell you how beautiful it seems to me when I am allowed to go to Jesus. After receiving Communion, I often feel as if my heavenly Father had taken me in his arms and pressed me to his heart. Then I can't speak because I'm so happy, but the Savior knows how much I love him."

Many bishops too were happy because the Holy Father had decided that young children should receive Holy Communion. Many of them had felt for years, just as the Pope had, that the ruling should be changed. And some of them, from time to time, had given permission to individual children to receive Holy Communion earlier than usual.

A bishop once told the Holy Father of something that happened in a parish in his diocese where he had gone to administer confirmation. While the bishop and the priests were dining, the doorbell rang, and a child asked to see the bishop. He went to the door to talk to her.

"Your Excellency, I would like to receive the dear Savior, but the pastor won't give him to me. Please say that I can receive him."

The bishop replied, "You are still too young, my child."

The little girl went into the church, and a priest who was also kneeling there in the dark heard her whispered prayer. "The bishop says that I'm still too young and that I don't know anything yet. But, Jesus, I know you so well. And I know a lot about you. I know how much you love us, because otherwise you wouldn't be here."

The next day the priest reported to the bishop what he had heard. The bishop knew then that the child was ready to receive our Lord, and he gave her permission to do so.

Once, during a large audience, a little girl slipped past the rows of pilgrims, ran straight to the Pope, and thanked him for having allowed her to receive

Holy Communion. Affectionately, the Holy Father bent down to the child.

"Whom did you receive?" he asked.

"Our Lord Jesus Christ."

"Was that our Savior in heaven or our Savior on earth?" was the next question. It was not an easy one to answer.

"It was the Savior who came down to the altar for me", the little girl replied.

"Then there is a Jesus in heaven and a Jesus on earth. But are there two Jesus Christs?" the Holy Father continued.

The child was silent for a moment. Then, to the great joy of the Holy Father, she found the right answer.

"No, Holy, Father," she said, "there is only one Jesus Christ. The Savior in the Host is the same as the One in heaven."

As soon as the Holy Father had flung open the doors of the tabernacle to children, groups of them began to come in pilgrimages to Rome to thank him personally for the great gift he had given them. Some of them traveled a long distance to see the Holy Father.

Less than two years after the Pope had issued his decree, a special train arrived from France bringing 400 French children who wished to thank the Holy Father. All types were represented. Some were from cities and some were from farms; there were rich children, and collections had been made to send poor ones too. They presented the Holy Father with an album containing the names of 134,330 boys and girls who had offered their Holy Communions for the Holy Father on his birthday, the Feast of Saint Joseph.

A French writer who talked with the children after they returned from Rome wrote: "I wanted to ask them how everything had gone. But that wasn't necessary, for they couldn't stop telling me of all they had seen. Everything had been wonderful. But the most beautiful sight of all—so beautiful that it had erased everything else from their minds—had been the Pope himself. They asked him to pray for them for special favors and had not been the least bit afraid of him. That would have been impossible because he had been so loving."

The Holy Father had such a great interest in children that he always found time to see them. A bishop standing in Saint Peter's Square one day noticed a ten-year-old boy who kept trying to get near him, but his parents would not allow him to do so. Finally the bishop raised his hand and beckoned to the child.

"Is it true, Your Excellency," the boy asked breathlessly, "that you are going to see the Holy Father?"

"Yes, son, that's true."

"Oh, Your Excellency, would you ask him something for me? Would you please ask him to pray that when I grow up, I can become a missionary?"

When the bishop saw the Holy Father, he gave him the message, and the Pope was so interested that he sent for the boy. In his private chapel, the Holy Father questioned the child.

"Now then, my son, you say you wish to be a missionary. That's a very serious thought, you know, because when one is a missionary, one has to make many sacrifices and perhaps even become a martyr."

"I know, Holy Father. But I do want to be a missionary and even a martyr, if it is God's will."

Then the Holy Father, convinced that the Lord had important plans for this child, knelt with him before the Blessed Sacrament, made the sign of the cross on his forehead, and solemnly prayed, "May the blessing of God descend upon you now and in the future, and may he assist you in your hour of danger."

Thirty years later, the same boy—then a missionary in China—died a martyr's death.

## XV

## A LIVING SAINT

AGAIN AND AGAIN one could hear these words: "Our Pope is a saint!" And those who were closest to the Holy Father could tell things of him that are heard only of the greatest saints. When the Pope heard that people were saying he could perform miracles, he remarked, laughing, "Now they are telling each other that I have begun to perform miracles, as if I had nothing else to do."

But it was true that Pius X did perform many miracles, for he had lived such a saintly life that God proved his pleasure in his servant by granting him this power. The people had every right to say that he was a saint.

Once a man with a completely paralyzed right arm came to one of the papal audiences. When the Pope approached him, the poor man begged, "Holy Father, heal me so that I can once more earn money for my family."

The Holy Father touched the man's arm. "Have faith in the Lord", he said. "He will heal you."

At that very moment new strength flowed through the paralyzed arm. And the man was able to move it as well as if there had never been anything wrong with it.

The Holy Father had turned and walked away, but the man wanted to tell him of the miracle, so he called out over the heads of the people, "Holy Father! Holy Father!" The Pope's eyes met his across the crowd of pilgrims, and, with a gesture, the Holy Father made the man understand that he should be silent.

A young Irish girl whose head was covered with sores begged her mother to take her to Rome. "The Savior has given his Apostle the power of working miracles", she said. "The Holy Father will surely be able to heal me."

Finally, the mother gave in to her daughter's urging and made a pilgrimage to Rome with her. When the Holy Father passed by, the girl begged him for his blessing and implored him to heal her. With great kindness, Pius X laid his hands on the girl's head, blessed her, and walked on. The girl cried, "Mother, I have been healed!"

When the bandages were removed from the child's head, there was not even a trace of the sores.

A girl in Rome had a foot ailment and for a year had been unable to walk. One day, someone gave her a sock that had belonged to the Holy Father. "Put it on", the friend said. "It will heal you."

Hardly had the girl pulled the sock up over her foot when she was healed. But when the Holy Father was told of this miracle, he only smiled. "That's a good joke", he said. "I wear my socks every day, and I always have pains in my feet."

A cardinal who was visiting the Pope told him of a sister—the cook in a children's hospital—who was losing her sight. The doctors were unable to help her, and the cardinal asked the Holy Father to pray for her.

"Oh, Sister Louise must not lose her sight!" the Pope exclaimed. "Otherwise, who would make the soup for the poor little ones?" He took off his glasses and handed them to the cardinal. "Here, bring her my glasses to wear and tell her that I am praying for her."

The cardinal brought the glasses to Sister Louise, and, as soon as she put them on, she was cured.

The Holy Father tried to prevent people from speaking of these miracles. "These things happen only because I am the successor of the apostles", he insisted. "I personally am not responsible." But the people knew that God was showing his approval of the Pope's personal sanctity.

A mother brought her lame daughter to the Holy Father and begged him to heal her.

"I cannot heal her", he replied. "Miracles can be worked only by God."

"If only you will ask God, Your Holiness", the mother replied.

Then the Holy Father leaned forward and whispered, "Have confidence. The Lord will heal your daughter." At that moment, the girl got up and walked, completely cured.

Miracles took place even in crowded rooms where the Holy Father could not reach the afflicted ones. A mother had brought her little boy to a papal audience in the hope that he would be cured. He had been deaf since birth, and all her hopes were centered in this meeting with the Pope. But the room was so crowded that she was unable to get near the Holy Father. Finally, full of discouragement, she began to weep. The Pope heard her, and he called out to her above the crowd, "Have confidence, have confidence!" At that moment the child began to hear.

The Pope was particularly moved at the sight of illness in children—his special friends. Once a couple came from Germany to see the Pope. They brought their little boy, who was unable to walk. When the Holy Father saw them, he walked over to where the child was lying, picked him up, and said, "Come, now, you must try to walk." The little boy ran to his parents, completely cured.

We are even told of cures that took place after the Pope's blessing had been received by letter or telegram. One man who needed legal assistance visited a famous lawyer in Milan but found him so upset that he was unable to concentrate on the case being explained to him. His little son was dying, and he was grief-stricken at the thought of losing him.

The man left the lawyer's office and decided to send a telegram to the Vatican to request the Holy Father's blessing on the child. About an hour later, a reply was wired from the Vatican; the Holy Father had sent a special blessing. The man went to the lawyer's home and showed the telegram to the sick child. The boy reached out a weak hand, grasped the paper, and immediately rose from his bed in perfect health.

Even in faraway countries such as India the news of the miracles performed by the saintly Pope was bringing hope and confidence to sufferers. In India, the mother superior of an orphanage had been seriously ill for years. She had consulted many doctors and had undergone surgery, but there was no sign of improvement.

The orphans who had just received their First Holy Communion decided to write to the Holy Father and ask him to help. "We have been privileged to make our First Holy Communion while we are still very young", they wrote. "We are very grateful to Your Holiness for this great blessing, and we wish to thank you. Our mother superior has been ill for fifteen years. . . . We would like so much to see her well again and humbly beg for this great blessing."

While the orphans awaited a reply from the Pope, the mother superior became much worse. She was not able to take any nourishment, and the sisters, seeing that she was dying, sent for a priest, who administered the last rites (Anointing of the Sick).

That evening, a telegram arrived from the Holy Father, granting his blessing. The mother superior was in her room when it arrived. She opened it and seemed to be filled with great happiness and confidence. She got up and dressed, ate dinner, and was able the following day to resume her work as superior.

A priest who had been called to Rome was hesitant to leave his elderly mother, who was seriously ill and seemed to be at the point of death. He decided not to go to Rome, but his mother would not hear of his staying with her.

"You must go to Rome," she insisted, "because if you ask the Holy Father to bless me, I will surely be cured."

So the priest went to Rome and arranged to have an audience with the Pope. As soon as Pius X walked into the room, he asked the priest how his mother was.

"She cannot live long, Your Holiness. She asked me to request for her your blessing."

The Holy Father lifted his eyes, prayed, and then patted the priest on the shoulder.

"I have prayed that she will be spared for many years to come", he said.

The priest wrote to his mother telling her of the Pope's prayer for her recovery, and soon he received word that his mother had been cured of her illness at the time the Pope had prayed for her.

The miraculous power God gave to Pius X extended also to the realm of prophecy. He often foretold events and read the secret thoughts of others.

Once when the Pope was administering the sacrament of confirmation to a group of children, he noticed that one girl was weeping.

"What is wrong, my child?" the Pope asked gently.

"Oh, Your Holiness, it is my parents. They have separated, and now I no longer have a home."

"Never mind, my child. When you go home, everything will be all right."

When she returned home, the girl learned that her parents had been reconciled.

On another occasion, a priest named Don Luigi,

who was about to have an audience with the Pope, wished to go to confession first. He found a priest who would hear his confession, but the confessor prolonged his instruction and advice until Don Luigi realized that he would be late for his audience with the Holy Father. Finally, he interrupted the confessor, requested absolution, and then rushed to the Vatican. Don Luigi had told no one of his plans to go to confession, but, when the Holy Father saw him, he said, "Don Luigi, you could have come without going to confession. But if you insist on doing so, you ought to give yourself a little more time."

A Trappist superior who had a serious problem to solve went to the Pope to ask his advice. But as soon as he knelt in front of the Pope, before he had said a word, the Holy Father gave him detailed instructions and advice on his problem.

Many people reported on the Pope's ability to read their thoughts and to know their secret actions.

A bishop who had been granted an audience with the Holy Father decided to bring along one of the priests of his diocese who had never been presented at the Vatican. The bishop introduced the priest to the Pope and told the Holy Father of the fine work this priest was doing for the Church in his home parish. The bishop was shocked when the Pope— usually so kind and fatherly—looked at the priest with sad and reproachful eyes. The bishop, puzzled and embarrassed, praised the priest all the more, even though he had no very definite knowledge of what the priest had accomplished. But the Pope still did not welcome the visitor in his usual warm and friendly way, for he knew that this priest secretly had an evil and disloyal attitude toward the Church. The bishop later discovered this, and he knew then why the Pope had acted as he had.

One day, two nuns who were afflicted with an incurable disease came all the way from Florence to ask the Pope's help.

"Holy Father, cure us", they begged.

"Why do you want to be cured?" he asked.

"So that we may work for the glory of God", they replied.

The Holy Father placed his hands on the nuns' heads, blessed them, and said, "Have confidence. You will be cured, and you will work—as you wish—for the glory of God."

Immediately they were restored to health. The Pope told them not to mention their cure to anyone, but those who were waiting outside could not help but be amazed. When the nuns had entered the audience room, they could hardly stand, yet they left in perfect health.

The coachman who had driven them to the audience was waiting outdoors to take them back to their convent. As they started to get in the coach, he cried, "No, no, sisters, I cannot take you. I already have passengers whom I must drive back to their convent. Either they or their corpses!" he added, thinking of the sick, feeble nuns he had driven from Florence.

"But we are the nuns you brought", they cried, and they had great difficulty convincing the coachman of their identity.

It is little wonder that the Catholics of the world cried out, even while Pius X was still living, "Our Pope is a saint!"

## XVI

## THE SERVANT'S REST

As the Pope's days on earth shortened and he continued to work unceasingly from morning till night, Cardinal Merry del Val often tried to persuade him to rest more.

"I am a servant in the Master's house", the Pope would reply. "When it is time, he will send my rest."

The year 1914 was a tragic one for the world. In that year the First World War began—the bloody war that was to rage throughout Europe for four years. It was the outbreak of this war that broke the heart of Pius X and led to his death.

For years, the Holy Father had prophesied that the war would come. "Woe to the world", he would say to those who were closest to him. "Something terrible is going to break over us. I see a great war coming." His sisters and his friends would try to comfort him, but he could not be roused from his sadness at the knowledge of what was to come.

"War is not expected, Your Holiness", Cardinal Merry del Val once said. "Things seem to be going well in the world."

"Before the end of 1914, war will come", replied the Pope firmly and sadly.

In 1911, when war broke out in Libya, the Holy Father said, "This is not the war I speak of. This is nothing compared with what is to come."

Again, in 1912, when there was war in the Balkans, many thought that this was the fulfillment of the prophecy. But the Holy Father only shook his head sadly. "This is not what I meant. Something far worse is going to overtake us."

In 1913, when the Brazilian ambassador to the Vatican was preparing to return to his own country, he had a farewell audience with the Pope.

"You are fortunate to be returning to your own

country", the Holy Father told him. "You will not be here to see the war that is soon to break out."

As 1914 and the dreaded war drew closer, Pius X became more and more oppressed with the thought of the terrible tragedy to come. Walking through the Vatican garden one day, he stopped before a shrine to Our Lady of Lourdes. Thinking of the war, he cried, "I am sorry for my successor. I shall not be here. *Devastated Religion*"—the name in Malachy's prophecy for the Pope to follow Pius X—"is almost here."

Even though the Holy Father was horrified by the knowledge of the catastrophe that was going to befall his children, he did not lose his feeling for their immediate needs. In those years just before the outbreak of the war, a large number of Italians were emigrating from their native land to other countries of Europe and to America.

The Pope knew the difficulties to be met by these people as they made their homes in a foreign land. He knew, above all, the dangers to their faith. In countries where the customs were strange, where they were without the consolation of priests who understood them and their language, there was danger that they might neglect the Faith in which they had been reared.

As bishop of Mantua, Pius X had been aware of these problems and had done everything possible to help the emigrants, even aiding them financially. He urged them to take the catechism, devotional books, and their baptismal certificates, and to hold fast to their religion in their new homes.

As Pope, Giuseppe Sarto had even greater concern for emigrants. In 1914, just a few months before his death, he established a training school for priests who would act as chaplains to these people by going with them to the new lands they had chosen. This was the greatest gift the Holy Father could give his people— their own priests who spoke their language and understood their customs, hopes, and fears.

Two months before the war began, Pius X met with his cardinals for the last time. The coming war was still not evident, but the Pope warned the princes of the Church that the battle was at hand. "There are men of skill and authority", he said, "who, foreseeing in their hearts the fate of their states and the destruction of human society, search for possible ways and means to prevent the cursed tumult and butchery of war. Their purpose is, indeed, a blessed one, but their success will be small unless desperate efforts are made to plant justice and love in the hearts of all men."

In June 1914, the event occurred that was to lead directly to the First World War. Franz Ferdinand, the heir to the Austrian crown, and his wife were murdered. When the Holy Father was informed of the murder, he moaned, "This is the beginning. Now more and more innocent blood will flow."

The Holy Father prayed and pleaded for peace. Day and night he knelt in prayer, often prostrating himself before the Blessed Sacrament to beg God's mercy. But he could not stem the tide; it was too late.

In desperation, the Holy Father wrote to the emperor of Austria. "I have not desired to speak to you through offices and embassies. My heart goes directly to your heart, and your father—he who represents Christ on earth—prostrates himself before you. I implore you to abandon this war and will not leave you till you give the order for peace as you gave the order for war. You gave the order for Serbia to be destroyed; you have now reduced Belgium to ashes. Am I not the shepherd of these lambs? I will not strike you down because I have given my life for you. But if *I* do not excommunicate you, it will be the curse of heaven that will fall upon your head. My dearest son, I bless you today because I am still your father. Tomorrow will be too late; you will be cursed."

But the letter never reached the emperor; it was delivered to one of the government officials, who did not forward it. So we shall never know what might have happened if the heart of the emperor had been moved by the plea of the Pope. The words of the Holy Father were in vain; the First World War had begun.

In the early days of the war, the Austrian ambassador sought out the Pope. "Holy Father," he begged, "bless our army."

But the Pope refused to give his blessing. "I bless only peace," he replied, "not war."

Eighteen days before his death, the heartbroken Holy Father—exhausted by his fruitless efforts—sent his last message to his children. He begged them to unite their prayers that God would grant peace. "We admonish the Catholics of the whole world to take refuge, full of confidence, at the throne of divine mercy", he wrote. "The clergy should lead the way by their example and should organize in their parishes public devotions and prayers that God will be moved to compassion and will extinguish as soon as possible the torches of war and will instill in those who are charged with the government of the people thoughts of love and peace, instead of hatred and war."

When the first tragic reports were brought back from the battlefront, Pius X wept like a father at the death of his children. "My poor, poor children", he would cry.

One of the sadder events of the Pope's life occurred at this time. Almost all the countries of Europe sent their seminarians from time to time to study in Rome. They lived there as brothers, praying and studying in the peaceful, scholarly atmosphere of the Eternal City. But, when the war broke out, these students were called home to their own countries for army duty. They were forced to abandon for a time—and, in some cases, forever—their hopes of becoming priests of God.

The seminarians came for a farewell audience with the Pope before leaving Rome. The Holy Father, with tears in his eyes, looked at these young men of all nations—French, German, Austrian—who would soon be facing one another on the battlefield. As he blessed them, he said, "Show yourselves worthy of the Faith you profess. In war do not forget mercy and compassion." Those who were closest to the Pope thought that this moment was the saddest and most difficult one for his fatherly heart to bear.

But Divine Providence spared Pius X from the worst days of the war. He saw only the beginning of that terrible, four-year ordeal; in August, death saved him.

On August 15, the news spread through Rome: "The Holy Father is seriously ill." Only a few days previously, he had received a group of pilgrims, but even then it was evident that he was exhausted. He had not made even a short speech. Neither had he walked about the room. He had sat nearly motionless on the papal throne while he gave his blessing to the pilgrims.

For two more days the Pope tried to continue his work, struggling weakly from bed to desk. But on August 19, it became clear that he was going to die. He resigned himself to the will of God and peacefully received the last rites. The Holy Father was eighty years old. He had lived the life of a saint, and now his Master was calling him home for his reward. There was no reason to mourn.

The bells of Saint Peter's sounded to announce to the people of Rome that the Holy Father was dying. All the bells of the city followed, calling the faithful to prayer for their Pope. Churches were filled with sorrowing people, and crowds gathered in Saint Peter's Square to pray. The Holy Father prayed, too, begging God's forgiveness for the sins of his life and for the terrible crimes of the war.

Cardinal Merry del Val, the Pope's loyal companion and assistant, stood beside him as he had during the eleven years of Giuseppe Sarto's reign. There were other cardinals present, too, and his faithful sisters, who had taken such good care of him during his days as country pastor, bishop, and cardinal.

The Holy Father made the sign of the cross and, just before he died, kissed the crucifix. On his face there was an expression of utter kindliness. His death, it was said, could not have been more peaceful. The Master's servant had at last earned his rest.

When the news of the Pope's death was announced, the people of Rome—and the people of the world—knew that they had lost a father. "A saint is dead." These were the words on the lips of many. "The war broke his heart." And the people kneeling in Saint Peter's Square, convinced that the Holy

Father was already with God, were pleading, "Saint Pius, pray for us."

The newspapers of the world—even those that traditionally criticized the Church—united in praise of the beloved Pius X. The sincere virtue and holy life of the Pope had edified the entire world.

The diplomats at the Vatican were deeply grieved at the loss of the Pope. One, a non-Catholic, wished to be transferred to another city because, he said, Rome would never be the same for him without the presence of Pius X.

The body of the Pope was placed in the throne room, and crowds of people—rich and poor, Catholic and non-Catholic, Italian and French, American and German—came to view the saintly features of Pius X for the last time.

On August 23, Pope Pius X was buried in the crypt of Saint Peter's, close to the grave of the first Pope. In front of the tomb was placed a metal plate on which these words were engraved:

POPE PIUS X

POOR AND YET RICH

GENTLE AND HUMBLE OF HEART

UNCONQUERABLE CHAMPION OF THE CATHOLIC FAITH

WHOSE CONSTANT ENDEAVOR IT WAS TO RENEW

ALL THINGS IN CHRIST

DEPARTED IN PIETY

ON THE TWENTIETH OF AUGUST, 1914.

## XVII

# PIUS X, SAINT OF OUR TIMES

As the body of Pope Pius X was laid to rest, one of the cardinals present said, "Pius X is dead, but he still lives on in the memory of the people and in the history of the Church. I have no doubt but that this part of the Vatican grotto will become a place of pilgrimage."

The tomb of the saintly Pope did soon become a place of pilgrimage. People came from all over to pray there and to attend Mass. For a little altar had been placed near the tomb so that the faithful could hear Mass and receive Holy Communion near the grave of the "Pope of the Eucharist".

Cardinal Merry del Val himself celebrated Mass there on the twentieth of each month—the day on which the Pope died—for the remaining sixteen years of his life. He celebrated Mass at the Pope's tomb for the last time just six days before his death.

Soon after the death of the Pope, his will was opened and read. He had written, "I was born poor, I have been poor all my life, and I shall die poor." And that was exactly how he died, having practically no possessions. In his will, the Holy Father asked the generosity of the Vatican in allowing a small monthly payment to be made to his sisters. They had served him well, and he wished them to be taken care of in their old age.

In his will, the Holy Father also specified that his body should be buried soon after death in the crypt of Saint Peter's Basilica.

Nine years after the death of Pius X, it was announced that a statue of him was to be placed in Saint Peter's Basilica. It has been traditional, after the death of a Pope, for the cardinals whom he had appointed during his reign to have a statue of him placed in Saint Peter's. This was usually arranged by the cardinals alone, but when the faithful learned

that there was to be a statue of their beloved Pius X,
they begged to have a part in it.

From all over the world, contributions poured in
from people who wished to help pay for the statue.
Large donations were received from the wealthy,
and the poor contributed the few pennies they could
afford. And so the statue represented the love and
gratitude of the millions of people who wished to
pay tribute to the Holy Father.

The statue is of white marble, and those who
knew the Holy Father say it is very true to life. It
portrays Pius X with arms outstretched in love and
self-sacrifice. Pope Pius XI, who unveiled the statue
in a ceremony at Saint Peter's, said at the time, "The
dead Pope still speaks; he really speaks; he speaks by
the marvellous simplicity of the whole work—a simplicity so much in accord with the humble life of the
glorified Pope. To all who look upon it, this monument is an encouragement to pray, to sanctify themselves, to pardon injuries, and to do good. This
monument is an honor that even the humble boy
of Riese could not refuse—in spite of his great
humility."

In 1935—the hundredth anniversary of the birth
of Pope Pius X—the Catholic world joyfully celebrated the memory of the great event and thanked
God for blessing the Church with such a saintly
leader. More and more people streamed to Rome to
visit the tomb of the Pope. Even the tiny village of

Riese was becoming a famous site as pilgrims visited the little house where Giuseppe Sarto was born, the simple church where he was baptized and served Mass, and the road to Castelfranco he had so often trod.

From the time of the death of Pius X, messages began to arrive at the Vatican from all over the world declaring the goodness of the dead Pope, telling of miracles performed both during his life and after his death, and begging that the Church take the necessary steps to declare him blessed. For this process of beatification must precede the canonization process, by which the Church declares someone a saint. The Roman cardinals themselves, as a group, had requested that these processes be started—an action which had never before been taken by the princes of the Church.

So the preliminary work was begun, and investigations were made in all the towns and cities where Pius X had lived. Every phase of his life was thoroughly studied, and those who had known him were questioned. The Church must be completely convinced of the person's sanctity before she raises him to the ranks of the blessed, and these investigations often go on for many years.

It was declared, after investigation, that Pius X had led a life of heroic virtue. But the Church still was not satisfied; she demanded that miracles be performed through the intercession of the person being investigated. God must show his approval of that person, says the Church, by performing miracles on his behalf. Then the Church will know that the one she holds up to her children as saintly did truly lead a saintly life close to God.

In the case of Pius X, it was not necessary to seek miracles. Letters poured in telling of miracles performed during the life of the Pope and after his death.

Two of these reported events were thoroughly investigated, scientifically examined, and finally declared to be genuine miracles. The only explanation for these events was divine intervention, and reports of them were placed in the records as official miracles.

One of the miracles, both of which took place after the death of the Pope, involved a French nun. She had a fatal disease of the hip and had been told by doctors that she had not long to live. One of the sisters in the convent was given a relic of Pope Pius X. She pinned it to the clothing of the sick sister and asked the other sisters in the convent to make a novena to the Pope.

They prayed fervently for the recovery of the patient but, by the end of the novena, she had become worse. They never lost confidence in Pius X and immediately began a second novena. But the patient grew worse every day, and the doctors warned the sisters that the case was hopeless.

Suddenly the sick sister sat up in bed and felt perfectly well, even though a few minutes before she had seemed to be at the point of death. The doctor was called. He was amazed at the change because when he had left the convent a short time before, he had warned the sisters that the patient would not live long. Two other doctors—who had examined the patient earlier and had agreed with the first doctor's diagnosis—were called, and neither of them could explain the cure. There was no trace of the disease; the sister was in perfect health.

The second miracle took place in Italy and also involved the curing of a sick sister who was expected to die at any moment. She had a fatal stomach disease, and all treatment had been in vain. The other sisters in the convent began a novena to Pius X. One day, the patient swallowed a small bit of material from the clothing of the Pope, and the disease immediately disappeared. The other sisters of the community were gathered in the chapel at the time, and they were shocked when they saw the cured sister—looking strong and well—walk in to join them.

The sister explained what had happened, and the doctor—who came a few minutes later—could find no sign of the disease. It was a complete cure, and the doctor swore to the investigators of the miracle that there was no possible physical explanation for it.

In 1951, thirty-seven years after his death, it was declared that Pius X should be known as Blessed

Pius X, in recognition of his heroic virtues and the miracles performed in his name. This ceremony of beatification took place on June 3—the same day on which Giuseppe Sarto had been baptized in the country church of Riese.

The bells of Rome rang out joyfully as Pope Pius XII pronounced the decision of the Church that the name of his predecessor had been placed among the ranks of the blessed.

Three years later, the world again looked to Rome, and many came from all over the world to be present at the solemn ceremony of canonization. Seldom has the Eternal City witnessed a celebration to compare with this one. So many people wished to attend the canonization that the ceremony had to be performed in Saint Peter's Square, which can hold a million people.

Blessed Pius X was declared a saint when Pope Pius XII solemnly proclaimed:

To the honor of the holy and indivisible Trinity; to the glory of the Catholic Faith and the dissemination of the Christian religion; by the authority of Jesus Christ and of his holy apostles Peter and Paul, and in our own name; after mature consideration and with fervent prayers for God's help; after consultation with our honorable brothers, the cardinals of the holy Roman Church, the patriarchs, the archbishops, and bishops here present in Rome; we decide and affirm that the late Pope Pius X is a saint, and as such we

enroll him in the roster of the saints. We decree that
his memory shall be celebrated each year on the day of
his death, namely, on the twentieth of August.

Pius X had been declared a saint of God, and it was
with great joy that his children could at last cry out,
"Saint Pius X, pray for us!"

It was a long road that Giuseppe Sarto had traveled. The majestic ceremony in Saint Peter's by
which he was given the highest honor of the Church
was an event never dreamed of by the farm boy of
Riese who had tended the family's vegetable plots
and helped his father carry the village mail.

The road had been long and winding and a difficult one to walk. But Giuseppe Sarto had walked it
with simplicity, humility, and resignation to the will
of God—all the way from the hard, stony highway
of Castelfranco, shoes on his shoulder, to the magnificent aisle of Saint Peter's, the three-tiered crown
on his head. Finally, with the outbreak of the war,
he had at last climbed his hill to Calvary. And he had
found Jesus Christ waiting.